THE
SECRET SISTERS
OF
FINNLEY FOREST

LORI A. REEVES

WESTBOW®
PRESS
A DIVISION OF THOMAS NELSON
& ZONDERVAN

WestBow Press books may be ordered through booksellers or by contacting:

WestBow Press
A Division of Thomas Nelson & Zondervan
1663 Liberty Drive
Bloomington, IN 47403
www.westbowpress.com
1 (866) 928-1240

Because of the dynamic nature of the Internet, any web addresses or links contained in this book may have changed since publication and may no longer be valid. The views expressed in this work are solely those of the author and do not necessarily reflect the views of the publisher, and the publisher hereby disclaims any responsibility for them.

Cover image titled a Childhood Idyll, by William-Adolphe Bouguereau, c 1900. License agreement by Image Envision,com.

All Scripture quotations are taken from the Authorized King James Bible.

Bear Track Icon made by Freepik from Flaticon.com

ISBN: 978-1-4908-3338-5 (sc)
ISBN: 978-1-4908-3340-8 (hc)
ISBN: 978-1-4908-3339-2 (e)

Library of Congress Control Number: 2014906369

Printed in the United States of America.

WestBow Press rev. date: 04/18/2014

DEDICATION

To my Lord and Savior Jesus Christ, the one who loved me, and gave Himself for me. The giver of Life and all good things. I thank You. To You, I bow my heart and knee and give You my allegiance.

Acknowledgements

First, I would like to say thank you to my wonderful husband, adventure partner, and best friend. We have been on many wonderful adventures together. I look forward to many, many more. Thank you for all your love, support, and encouragement. This book would not have been possible without you. You are my knight in shining armor, and I am very thankful that we are living happily ever after.

Pastor Daniel Buchanan, thank you for the many years of instruction, guidance, and sound biblical preaching. You are a living example of God's love, and your prayers are more valuable to us than silver and gold.

"How beautiful are the feet of them that preach the gospel of peace, and bring glad tidings of good things!" (Romans 10:15)

Lita Belk, the best English teacher on the planet and the smartest girl in the family! Thank you for all your help and hard work.

Debby Handy and Heather Hutchens, thank you for being so kind and gracious every time I shoved an updated copy of the manuscript at you to proofread. Thank you for the encouragement.

Elizabeth Wagoner, you are such a talented girl. Thank you for your technical help with the cover.

Dr. Scott Phillip Stewart at Christian Author Services, thank you so much for your kindness and excellent editorial contribution.

Finally, to my father Albert Adams, I'm so thankful you came to trust the Savior. You loved your little girl to the fullest the last year of your life. I love you, Daddy, and I'll meet you by the stream….

Luke 8:17 For nothing is secret, that shall not be made manifest; neither *any thing* hid, that shall not be known and come abroad.

CONTENTS

Cast of Characters

Eve
While walking through the woods,
this lonely young girl discovers a new friend,
begins an adventure that reveals many secrets,
and changes the destiny of two kingdoms.

Dawn
Eve's newfound friend.

Brin
Lord of the kingdom of Peacehaven.
Captain of the soldiers from the village of Garland.

Cook
Keeper of the house of Brin and Eve.

Magi
Lord Brin's exceptional warhorse.

Johanan
Lord Brin's charge and protégé.

Albert
Lord of the kingdom of Peacehaven.
Captain of the soldiers from the village of Blain.

King Amasa
Good king of the kingdom of Peacehaven.

Lucian
An evil advisor to King Amasa,
who plots to overthrow the kingdom.

Captain Karl
Lucian's reluctant, misguided captain.

Sir Marcus
Leader of the woodsmen.
Banished from the kingdom of Avery.

Mikael
Teenage son of Sir Marcus.

Artemas
A skilled archer and noble leader among the woodsmen.

Gilbert
A skilled slinger and noble leader among the woodsmen.

Nicolas the Hermit
A mysterious and legendary figure of Wylderland.

SETTINGS

Peacehaven: The noble, yet troubled, kingdom of King Amasa.

Finnley Forest: A pleasant woodland between the villages of Garland and Blain where Eve and Dawn first meet.

Garland: A country village settlement not far from the home of Brin.

Blain: A country village settlement not far from the home of Albert.

Cliffs of Dove: The north-west most corner of the kingdom of Peacehaven, where Lucian tempts Albert.

Wylderland: A dark foreboding forest. The eastern border of Peacehaven between Peacehaven and Avery.

Hidden Village: The home of the exiled woodsmen within the forest of Wylderland.

Avery: Peacehaven's eastern neighbor and ally.

The Unexpected Meeting

In the fifteenth year of the reign of King Amasa, in the kingdom of Peacehaven, there lived two little girls. The older was ruddy and plump with long brown hair that fell in curls down her back. Her name was Eve. The younger was thin and frail yet fair as the morning, with long, straight golden hair. Her name was Dawn.

Both girls lived in the vast expanse of Finnley Forest and had not met until one day when, in the providence of God and the time was right, everything changed.

While walking through the forest as she often did, Eve ventured a bit farther than she ever had before and happened upon a place where two small streams met. The day was beautiful. A soft, gentle breeze carried the fresh smell of spring through the air, making her walk especially enjoyable. The woods were alive with the singing of birds, the buzzing of bees, and the occasional chatter of a chipmunk. In fact, it was such a lovely day that Eve lost all sense of her normal boundaries and wandered much farther than she intended.

Suddenly, she caught a glimpse of something golden dancing in the wind. She squinted and thought she saw the form of a girl, smaller than herself, just up ahead.

"Hello! Hello!" She called out after the form.

Instead of responding or drawing closer, the obscure little form simply vanished in the shadow of the trees. Eve questioned in her heart whether she had actually seen a little girl or not. After calling out again and again with no sign or answer, puzzled and bewildered, Eve turned and hurried toward home.

Home for Eve was a comfortable cottage at the edge of the forest that she shared with her kind father, Brin, and a motherly housekeeper they simply called Cook. Eve had never known a real mother, just the meek and gentle Cook who had always loved and treated her as a daughter.

Eve was very happy at home except for missing her father who was often gone for weeks at a time. It was bliss, however, when he returned because he never failed to shower her with so much love and attention that it made his absence seem like but a shadow.

Home for Dawn was a different matter altogether. Her dwelling consisted of a dismal little thatch-roofed shack that better resembled a mud hut than a proper cottage. She shared the humble abode with her father, Albert, a hard, bitter man with a violent temper who kept much bottled up inside and spent little time at home. She had no mother and no caring housekeeper, no one to tend to her, play games, or teach her how to care for a home, or cook, or do any of the things that Cook had taught Eve. Yes, Dawn's home life was very different from Eve's.

Dawn spent many lonely hours while her father was away, and when he returned, he treated her more like a servant than a daughter. When he was gone, she thought she would die of loneliness, but, when he was home, she longed for him to go away. Dawn spent much of her time in agonizing fear. In some strange way, the loneliness had become a faithful companion that Dawn preferred to the unexplainable tensions that prompted her father's sudden violent outbursts over the smallest of matters. She could bear being alone better than being in fear. Through it all, she did her best to please her father, and earn his favor, for that's all a little girl longs for, isn't it? No matter how Albert treated her, he was still her father, and all she wanted was to please him and make him happy so that maybe someday he would be proud of her and love her with a father's unconditional love.

So Dawn did her best to obey Albert's rules, even though she really didn't understand them – rules such as: never go far from the house or open the door to anyone. If she was ever seen outside, she wasn't to talk to anyone. In fact, if she could help it, she was to avoid letting others discover her at all. It was such a strange, hard, lonely life for a child, but Dawn tried her best to be obedient because he was, after all, her father.

The next day, after enjoying a nice lunch with Cook, Eve decided once again to go for a walk in the forest. She had such a lovely time the day before, and, besides, she couldn't stop thinking about her recent adventure and that maybe, just *maybe*, she really had seen another little girl. So, blessed with another beautiful early spring day, a curious heart, and an adventurous spirit, off she went.

When Eve finally reached the spot where she thought she had seen something the day before, she looked around ever so closely. Then she made her way farther and farther, as quiet as a little mouse. Suddenly, after rounding a bend in the brook, Eve's heart dropped and her breath caught. Ahead, squatting down at the edge of the stream, was a real live golden-haired girl – the very same little girl Eve had seen the day before. She was pale and terribly thin, yet her blond hair was shining like the noonday sun. The girl had a small frame, and Eve could tell she was at least a few years younger than herself.

I did see a little girl! Eve thought to herself.

Eve couldn't quite make out what the girl was doing. She took a step closer and saw that the girl was so interested in something in the water that she was oblivious to the world around her and totally unaware of Eve's presence.

Instead of calling out to her, Eve approached her very softly so as not to scare the girl off again before she could get close enough to introduce herself properly.

When she was within a few feet of the little girl, she said, "Hello there."

Startled, as if from a sound sleep, Dawn turned to see who had spoken to her and drew her leg back as if to jump up and run, but after squatting for a while she did not quite have the full use of her legs and slipped on the muddy creek bank. She flung her arms out like a rag doll and fell sprawling feet first into the water.

"I'm sorry I scared you," Eve said, hardly knowing what to say after the awkward calamity she had just caused. "I didn't mean to. I would have called to you from back there, but I didn't want you to run away again like you did yesterday. My name is Eve. What's yours?"

The obviously shaken and now quite soggy little girl sat silent for a moment before finally blurting out, "I'm not supposed to talk to anyone. No one's supposed to see me."

"Well, I see you," Eve replied. "Besides, I'm just a little girl like you. It's not like I'm a grownup. What does it hurt if you talk to me?"

"I- I don't know," Dawn stammered. "I never thought about meeting another little girl," she added as she got to her feet in the shallow water. "I would so love to have someone to talk to because I do get lonely." Then she blushed and said, "Oh! I'm sorry. Where are my manners? My name is Dawn. I'm very glad to meet you, Eve. I'm sorry I ran away yesterday."

"That's all right," Eve said, shrugging. "You were just doing as you were told, I guess. What were you looking at in the water before I startled you so?"

"All the different colors."

"Colors of what?"

"Just all the different colors the sun makes in the water. Come here, and I'll show you."

Eve moved to the edge of the stream where Dawn was standing, and both girls peered into the water at the dazzling array of colors. For most of that afternoon, Dawn shared with Eve how she saw the world around her—reflections on the water, shadows cast by the evening sun, and a thousand different shades of green in the leaves of the trees as their branches danced in the wind against the clear blue of the sky. Dawn saw things that Eve had never noticed or even thought of before and found beauty in even mundane things that had escaped her eyes.

Maybe all the hours she spent alone had sharpened her senses, but Eve recognized right away that her newfound friend had a special gift, the ability to find the hidden splendor in the most ordinary parts of God's creation.

The two little girls talked and giggled until they began to notice how the time had slipped away.

"Oh dear!" Eve cried. "I must be getting back. Cook will be worried about me."

"Can you come back tomorrow?" Dawn asked. "I'm not supposed to be this far away from home, but it's been so long since I've had anyone to talk to, and I've had such fun."

"I will do my best," Eve said. "I'm sure Cook won't mind. My father is gone, and she takes care of me while he is away."

"My father is away, too, but I am all alone."

"Would you like to come home with me? Cook will be kind to you and give you a wonderful meal and—"

"Oh no," Dawn interrupted with a cry. "I mustn't meet anyone! Father says I'm not to speak to anyone and, if I can, not even to let anyone see me. Please don't tell anyone about me. If we could just keep this our own secret—no grownups, then everything just might be all right. My father would be very displeased if any big people found out about me."

"All right," Eve said, nodding her agreement. "It'll just be our secret. We can be *secret* friends. And while my father is away, I will come everyday to where the two streams meet and join you. How does that sound?"

"Oh, I would love that very much. My father is away a great deal of the time, and when he is, I spend my time in the forest here. I promise that when he is gone, I also shall come to the stream to meet you. Thank you, Eve. I've never had a friend before."

"It's going to be great," Eve replied. "We will call ourselves secret sisters."

"Oh, that's wonderful!" Dawn squealed with joy. "Secret sisters. I have been so lonely and now, in one day, I have discovered a friend and a sister all at once."

The two girls chatted for a while of the joys of their newfound friendship and then, with a parting hug and a promise for the morrow, headed each to her own home. But just as Dawn was about to lose sight of Eve she turned round and cried out, "Don't forget. Meet me by the stream!"

As Eve walked, she mused in her heart about her new friend and how natural a fit the kinship was. *Today is a very special and blessed day,* she thought to herself. Little did she realize at that moment that her life had changed forever.

Dawn was overjoyed and skipped toward the shack she called home, feeling happier than she could ever remember. A *friend*—she had found a friend! And not only a friend, for Eve had called them *secret sisters.*

"Secret sisters!" Dawn kept repeating. She loved the sound of those words.

FATHER'S RETURN

The next afternoon, the girls met again as promised. Eve had saved part of her lunch and shared it with Dawn. What a splendid time they had, splashing in the stream, chasing each other, playing games of their own making.

They met the next day, and the day after that, and many days following. The immediate bond the girls shared only grew stronger by the day. Every day Eve shared a portion of her lunch with Dawn, and as the days passed she saw her friend gain new strength.

Then one day Eve went to the stream and Dawn wasn't there. Eve called and called but no answer came. Finally, after a long and disappointing wait, Eve sadly made her way back home.

As the cottage came into view, however, she caught a sight that made her heart leap with joy. Standing just outside the kitchen door was her father Brin with his warhorse Magi, and Cook.

"Father! Father!" she cried. "You've come home at last!" She ran and jumped into his arms for one of his long, tight hugs.

"My, my, who is this beautiful young woman?" he said, looking her over. "You remind me of my little girl. But she is just a child, and you are a fine young lady."

"Oh, Father, you know it's me!"

"Well, well, so it is you! How did my little girl grow up so fast? From the kiss of the sun on your cheeks, I believe you've been spending time outdoors. Tell me now, what have you been doing while I was away?" Brin asked as he unpacked Magi.

"Well—" Eve began to say.

"Well," Cook interrupted, "she runs off every day taking part of her lunch with her and comes home all worn out."

"Is that so?" Brin chuckled as he began rubbing the sides of his very tired horse.

"Oh, Father!" Eve began. "I've had the most wonderful time. I have a new friend, and we meet every day and play and talk and have the grandest adventures together. Oh my!" Eve exclaimed, with a sudden change of countenance. "I forgot I wasn't supposed to tell anybody, but I was so excited to see you, and well, I can tell everything to you, can't I, Father?"

As Eve continued talking, Brin stopped rubbing Magi, and his smile faded into an expression of grave concern.

"Yes, of course, you can trust your father, my dear," he said. "You can tell me everything. Who is this newfound friend of yours?"

"Her name is Dawn. We've become the closest of friends; even though she is two years younger than I, that doesn't seem to matter really. Instead, it has only seemed natural somehow."

At that statement, Brin's look of concern turned to a look of fear, and his tone sharpened a bit and his deep-set eyes fixed firmly on the face of Eve. "Where did you meet this Dawn?"

"In the forest, where the two streams meet toward the south."

"And what of her family?" continued Brin.

"She lives mostly alone; that's how we get to play so much. She only has her father, and he is away much of the time like you. She told me once that her mother and sister died of the fever when she was five. I think she must be very poor, for I take her part of my lunch each day. She was very pale and thin when we first met, but she seems to be recovering a bit now. I'm afraid the portion of my lunch may be most of the food she gets."

"Tell me," Brin asked, "what does this new friend of yours look like?"

"She is small, sort of frail like I said, but she is very beautiful with long blond hair and the bluest eyes, the color of the sky in spring."

"And you say she is a couple of years younger than you?"

"Yes."

"And she has only a father who is away much of the time?"

"Yes."

"Could it possibly be...?" Brin said as he faded off into his own thoughts."

"Could it be *what*, father?" Eve asked as she studied her father's face, fear growing in her heart.

"Tell me, Eve, when was the last time you saw your friend?"

"It was only yesterday, after lunch. I was supposed to meet her again today, and I went to the stream where we play, but she never came. She has always been there. I wonder if her father has come home just as you have come home."

"Maybe he has," Brin replied. "But for now, help me with Magi. He needs a good brushing and rub down, and some extra loving care from my little lady. He has traveled many leagues and is very tired."

"I will take extra special care of him for you, Father. Besides, I have missed him almost as much as I have missed you! Almost, but not quite!" Eve added with a grin. And at that she led the horse toward the barn to pet and spoil him as only a little girl can.

When she reached the barn, Brin turned to Cook. "Did you know of this?" he asked.

"No sir! Only that she never finished her lunch and went off to play." Cook looked down at her feet as if thinking back on it. "I did notice the child was happier than she had been in a very long time. She didn't seem to mind your being gone as she had, and she didn't seem as lonely. She would wake early, work hard, and have all her chores finished in time to help with lunch. Then she would go off to play and be home before dinner. When I asked her about her time away, she would always reply that she had been playing in the woods, having fun. She seemed well content, and, as you can see, she looks very healthy and strong, so I felt all was well. I am truly sorry, sir. I should have questioned the child further; I should have done more to—."

"Peace, Cook," Brin said, cutting her off. "It may be that all is well. I just wonder.... Do you think it is possible?"

"Sir, I do not know. We must needs seek the Lord's guidance, I feel."

"Indeed, we must. The time may be drawing nigh."

"Dear Lord, protect the children," was all Cook could whisper.

"Yes, Lord protect us all," Brin whispered in reply.

HOME AFTER DARK

Darkness had fallen once again before Dawn could reach her home deep in the Finnley Forest. But Dawn didn't mind. She was now used to walking home in the dark. She never got lost. Her keen eye knew every inch of the path, every hanging tree limb, every rock, and every vine along the way. Theirs was a friendly forest, and the light of the stars above was all she needed to guide her safely home.

Dawn's heart was full of joy, and for the first time since her mother and sister had died, she was content. She felt as if her special bond with her secret sister had somehow filled that sad, empty hole in her heart.

As she walked, she thought of gathering some grape vines and weaving two crowns – one for her and one for her friend – so they could be proper princesses.

I could pick some daisies and Queen Anne's lace and weave them into the front for jewels. That would make such beautiful crowns! Then we could rebuild the castle that Eve knocked over when she slipped on a rock and fell backwards into it.

Both girls had laughed so hard they cried.

If we build it closer to the stream next time, Dawn thought, *we could dig a moat that the water would fill. I will try to get our crowns made in the morning before I go to meet Eve. It will be a grand surprise! That should make her very happy.*

Dawn made her plans in her mind as she came to the edge of the trees at the clearing where the shack she called home stood, and her heart fell when she saw the light of a candle flickering in the window. She glanced quickly at the lean-to that served as a barn and, sure enough, there stood her father's horse. All her joy and contentment faded in a moment. Dawn's heart filled with fear and she nearly stumbled from the sickness that gripped the pit of her stomach. It was dark, and she was not home. She was in deep trouble, and she knew it. How long had her father been home? That was the question. If he hadn't been there long his anger might not be so bad. But if he had, she knew his rage would have grown to a boil.

As she approached the shack she prayed, "Please, Lord, don't let him have been here long." She stepped through the door, and trying her best to sound glad to see him and hide her fear, said, "Hello, Father, how good it is to see you."

But as she spoke she saw his face, his dark eyes black and glassy. She knew right away he had been waiting for some time.

"Where have you been?" Albert asked through clinched teeth as he stepped toward her.

"Just in the woods, Father," Dawn answered as she took a step back.

"You know the rules. You know better than to wander so far from home. How many times must I tell you? I have been here watching and waiting since early afternoon. You have blatantly disobeyed me!" By this time Albert's voice had risen to a fevered pitch. "Do you have any idea what you have put me through? Of all the reckless, selfish, and foolish things to do. I ask so little of you! After all I have done for you, this – *this* – is how you repay me?! With your childish disobedience? What have you *really* been doing?"

With that, the dam broke. A river of pent-up anger and frustration gushed forth, and there was no holding it back.

Voices in the Dark

That ungrateful child! After all I've done for her. After all I've sacrificed. Maybe Lucian was right. Am I not rightfully called "Lord" Albert ? I could have been living at my estate in Blain, but now that place falls to ruin while I have been hiding like a coward in these wretched woods all this time. She doesn't realize what I've given up for her, nor does she care.

As Albert rode through the night, his twisted thoughts raced faster than his galloping horse. At last, his muddled mind rested on a memory, one of Lucian, and the strange encounter that had haunted him nearly every day since. Though Albert tried ever so hard to dismiss them, Lucian's words ate at him like a cancer and pricked his weary mind like a festering sore that would not heal.

Albert and his men were working the outermost western edge of the kingdom near the white cliffs of Dove when the meeting took place. They had camped for the night and after building a fire, the watches were set.

Albert was restless despite the weariness of the road. He was tired to the bone and, more than that, he was spent. Utterly spent, like a bottle drained of all but the last few drops.

"I need a walk," Albert said, as he got up and strolled along the edge of the cliffs.

His mind wandered once again to memories of his wife. How he missed her still. Had it been three years or 30? He couldn't tell. He found it was the little things that he missed the most — the touch of her small soft hand clinging to his, the sound of her singing as she cooked, and the smell of her hair as she lay on his shoulder. When Albert was away on the king's business, he so loved the comfort of knowing she would always be home waiting for him. And then there was his baby girl. He had been so proud to have a daughter to love and protect. A daughter who would one day dote over him and give him grandchildren in his old age.

But now all that was gone, had vanished like a vapor, slipped through his fingers and drifted far, far from his reach. To Albert's broken heart neither life nor death seemed fair. Over and over, he thought of the day when he rode home to find that everything had changed, his beloved wife and child were gone forever.

As he thought about it, the weight of grief came crushing in on him afresh. Then his constant companion, bitterness, sprang up like an artesian well.

Why did my family have to die? Why did I have to lose them and the other child live? I don't understand. I tried to do right. I took her in. I protected her. And look what happened. What good is there in doing right?

While Albert traveled down that bitter road in his mind he lost all awareness of his surroundings. When he finally came to himself, he realized he had entered a hidden cove of some kind among the rocks that was bordered by a thick stand of trees straight ahead of him.

"I should be getting back," he said out loud. Then suddenly a hauntingly familiar voice came from somewhere among the trees.

"Great and mighty Lord Albert, is it worth it?" At once Albert snapped to attention and drew his sword.

"Who are you? How do you know who I am?"

"I know many things," the voice responded, except this time it seemed to come from a different direction.

Albert's heart was pounding. "Show yourself!" he shouted.

"All in due time," came the answer. "But first, pray tell, answer the question. Has it been worth it?"

"Worth *what?*" Albert asked.

"Has it been worth all the heartache and pain? Losing your own family, only to be forced to raise a child who does not belong to you. Then someday, after you have made all the sacrifice and done all the work, she will be returned to her real father who will reap all the benefits. While you, my dear Lord Albert, will surely be cast aside and forgotten. Like some obscure vision in the night, all of your efforts will soon fade from memory, unwelcome and unwanted."

"What are you talking about?" Albert asked, but his ragged voice was low and shaky. He wondered who it was who knew the thoughts of his troubled heart and was speaking as if he had read Albert's mind.

"You know precisely what I am talking about. I know who you keep. I also know the king is but using you. He cares not for the suffering that you have endured. He wishes only to satisfy his own selfish will. A king like that doesn't deserve such devotion as you have shown. What benefit is there for you – you who have lost so much? Has the king shown the least bit of sympathy? No! You deserve better treatment. You deserve someone who appreciates all your efforts, but do you receive it? No! You are only expected to give more. How much more do you have to give, honorable Lord Albert?"

What had begun as a veiled and mysterious encounter now broke upon Albert's mind clear as the noonday sun.

"I know who you are, Lucian! Come out into the open!"

"Why? So you can arrest me? I do nothing wrong here. I simply wish to talk to you and point out some things that merit your consideration. You have been burdened long enough with the care of that child. I offer to you your freedom. I will take charge of the child and care for her most graciously until such a time as this whole twisted matter can be seen in a clearer light."

"Yes, I know you want the child," Albert answered roughly in a feeble attempt to display more confidence in his feigned voice than he felt in his trembling heart. "But you shall not have her,"

"Just think about it," Lucian said. "That is all I am asking. I have been sorely misunderstood and harshly misjudged. I wish the child no harm at all. Nay, but I wish only to care for her so as to prove to the king that he was wrong about me all along; it was all just a big misunderstanding. Again, all I am asking is that you think about it." Then, like a ghostly shadow from an unseen world, Lucian was gone, nowhere to be found

As Albert replayed the scene in his mind, he thought to himself: *Lucian wants to keep the child only to prove a point. So maybe I should let him.*

A Dark Discovery

The next day Eve asked her father if she may please go see if Dawn was at the stream. "Yes," he answered reluctantly, "but hurry home for I have missed my little girl while on my travels."

"I will come back soon," she told him. "I have missed you, too; I just want to look for my friend."

"Go and see if you can find her, but be sure and take some food with you, the roast mutton from last night's meal, with some extra cheese and bread."

"Oh thank you, Father!" she exclaimed, then ran into the house, gathered the items together in a cloth, and bounced back out the door. Eve ran as fast as she could to the meeting place of the two streams hoping all the way to find her special friend waiting by the water as she had so many times before. She would explain that she had shared their secret with her father but then prove everything would be all right because he had sent her a feast. But she was only to be disappointed. Her secret sister was nowhere to be found.

"Dawn! Dawn!" she cried. "Where are you?" But her echo in the hollow forest was the only reply. Anxious fear crept into her little heart, though she wasn't quite sure why. Maybe it was the grave look on her father's face the day before or maybe it was something much more. It was as though she was somehow connected to Dawn and could sense she was in trouble, and then the thought came crushing in on her: *She needs me!*

With the revelation came direction. "I must get Father, for something is wrong. Something is terribly wrong." Without hesitating further, Eve turned and ran home, feet and heart pounding, crying, "Father! Father!"

Brin heard her desperate cries long before she reached the small clearing in which their cottage was nestled. Alarmed, he bolted down the path and met Eve running. He grabbed her up into his arms.

"Eve, darling, what's wrong? Are you all right? What's wrong?"

"I don't know, Father; Dawn is not at the stream again today, and I have this awful feeling that she is in trouble and needs me. I can't explain it. I just know something bad is wrong, and we must find her!" At this, Eve was in sobs. Brin held her tight in his arms as he made his way back to the cottage.

"Be still, my daughter, we will find her. And if she is in trouble, we will help. Now dry those tears and be strong. You must help me saddle Magi."

By this time Cook had appeared by the door with great distress tugging at her face. Brin only looked at her. No words needed to be said. Both knew in their hearts it was "her."

"You must needs tell her," Cook said at last.

"Yes, the day has come at last. Eve and I will go look for the child. Pray for us that we shall find her before it's too late."

"I shall," Cook replied. "God's speed." At that, Eve came leading the war horse Magi from the barn, and Brin stepped away to fetch the saddle. Cook turned and stepped inside, grabbed her well-worn Bible, knelt by her bed, and prayed with a fervent heart.

"Tell me again where your meeting place is," Brin said.

"Toward the south where the two streams come together."

"Then that is where we will begin our search."

When they reached the meeting place, Brin halted. He could see right away the evidence of the girls' afternoons of play – trampled grass, broken limbs, and piles of rocks that had once been grand castles. For a moment he could envision the two girls laughing and playing without a care in the world. "Which is as it should be," he whispered to himself.

Once again Eve called out to her friend, but no answer came.

"Which way to her cabin?" asked Brin.

"She comes from that direction," Eve answered as she pointed to a path that ran beside the stream. Brin shouted "Forward!" to Magi and off they went. The path followed the stream for a bit before turning slightly north. It looked to Brin to be no more that a hart path until his keen eye caught a glimpse of a long blond strand of hair clinging to a branch. He slowed Magi's pace, and they scanned the woods as they followed the trail, with Eve calling out to Dawn all the while. Eve was amazed at the great distance Dawn had been traveling everyday just to meet and play.

"It must have been very dark by the time she made it home each day," Eve said. "I had no idea. She must be very brave."

"Yes," Brin answered, "she must be very brave indeed. From here on, my daughter, we mustn't call out anymore. We must simply look for what we shall find."

"But, Father, why—?" she started to ask.

Brin interrupted. "You must trust me. Do you trust me?"

"Why of course I trust you. I trust you with my life, Father."

"Indeed you have, my daughter. Now let's see if we can find your friend, but quietly."

With that, a new fear arose in Eve's heart. Why did her father speak that way? And why couldn't she call out to her friend? So much she didn't understand, yet she chose to trust the one she knew loved her dearly.

After what seemed like an eternity, the path lightened ahead. Slowly and quietly, they proceeded. Up ahead in a small clearing, they saw the feeble, little shack Dawn called home. *This looks more like a bandit's outpost,* Brin thought. Stopping Magi under the cover of the trees, Brin dismounted and put his finger to his lips to remind Eve to be very quiet. Then unsheathing his sword, he stealthily approached the shack. Eve couldn't believe her eyes as she watched her father, quiet as an owl in flight and nimble as a cat stalking its prey, move toward the shack. In spite of her fear, her heart swelled with pride and admiration as she determined that her father must be in "work" mode.

No one in sight; not a sound; no horse in the makeshift stable. Brin reached the side of the shack and had no trouble peering inside through one of the many holes in the wall. The inside was a worse mess than the outside. A table overturned, a chair smashed to pieces, things strewn all around. Then amidst the scattered debris, his eye fell on something golden lying on the floor in the corner. Behind the table, on the floor, was what looked to be a pallet, and on the pallet lay the small crumpled body of a bruised and battered little girl.

Panic welled in Brin's heart. "Father God, have mercy on this child!" He rushed through the door and knelt down beside the little girl. She awoke at the sound of his coming and peered up through red swollen eyes. Brin's heart was crushed as he saw a fresh wave of terror and confusion sweep across her timid face. Bending down, Brin gently stroked her golden hair and whispered softly, "It's all right, little one. It's going to be all right now. I'm not going to hurt you; no one will ever hurt you again. I will see to that."

At this, Eve came running in crying, "Dawn! Dawn!"

At the sound of her friend's voice, the terror on Dawn's face gave way to peace, and a weak smile crossed her swollen lips as she faded off into sleep once more.

Eve, sobbing now, said, "Oh, Father, what has happened? Will she be all right?"

"Be still, my daughter. You must be brave, as brave as your little friend traveling alone in the dark woods. Help me wrap her in this blanket; we must keep her warm. And, my daughter, pray."

"Yes, Father, I will try to be brave, and I will pray."

"Good," Brin replied.

Carefully, they wrapped the little girl in the tattered remains of a dirty old blanket, and Brin carefully carried her to Magi. With Dawn in one arm, he mounted the saddle and then pulled Eve up behind him. Quickly, they retraced their steps and soon made their way back to the comfort of their little cottage.

Cook was waiting at the door as they came up. Her eyes were red and her cheeks wet with tears from praying in earnest. "Praise be to God!" Cook cried. "You found her!"

"Yes, indeed, we have. Your prayers have been answered," Brin said as he lowered his bundle into the waiting arms of Cook. "Albeit, we are still in need of God's mercy it would seem." As Brin spoke the blanket gave way and Cook saw firsthand the frail little form and the marks of her torment.

"Oh, my poor child!" Quickly, Cook carried the little bruised body through the open door and laid her on her own bed.

Dawn awoke again as Cook stroked her matted hair. Cook did her best to soothe the child's fears as she cleaned her wounds and washed her face. As Dawn began to recover a bit, she finally spoke. "Would it be too much to ask for a drink of water? If so, I would be very content to suck on that rag."

"Oh, my dear! Yes, of course you can have all the water you are able to drink!" And with that Cook gave her a drink and then asked, "Do you feel as if you could have a bite to eat?"

"I think so," Dawn replied. "I haven't eaten since two days ago when Eve shared her lunch with me."

Cook sprang to her feet and set about making a tray of food for the child. From the morning meal, she laid out on a wooden tray a wheat cake, with fresh butter and honey, two good sized pieces of cheese with a boiled egg, an apple, and a handful of grapes. She placed it beside Dawn on the bed. "Well now," Cook said, "what do you think you would like to eat?"

"Would it be too much to ask for half of that piece of cheese?" Dawn asked sheepishly.

"Half a piece?" Cook said. "Is that all you want, half a piece?"

"Do you mean I could have the *whole* piece?" Dawn asked, eyes wide with amazement.

"The whole piece, why yes, of course you can have the whole piece. In fact, you can have the whole tray. This tray of food is for you. All of it!"

"I've never seen so much food at one time before," Dawn confessed.

Tears welled in Cook's eyes. "Now you can see it, and eat as much of it as you would like, or as much as that small frame of yours will allow." Cook then slid the tray closer to Dawn and left her to enjoy her meal.

Outside, Cook met Eve and Brin coming out of the barn.

"How is she?" Brin asked.

"She's taken quite a beating, but what seems to ail her most is lack of food and water. The poor child is half starved. If she continues to eat, her strength should return within a few days."

"I don't know if we have a few days," Brin replied.

Startled, Eve asked, "What are you talking about, Father? Why can Dawn not just live here with us? I can help Cook extra and, besides, it only seems natural for her to be here. You could be *her* father, too, and she could be my sister. We would be a family together."

"My dearest daughter," Brin replied as he bent on one knee facing her, "nothing would please me more, but, there is much that you do not yet know, and I fear the time is drawing nigh that you must be told. Much is about to change. But this is neither the time nor the place. We shall talk when your friend is a bit stronger and able to listen as well. But, for now, you must trust me, and help Cook care for your friend. Our Heavenly Father will take care of everything. Now, you go and see to your friend and comfort her. Assure her all shall be well and that she will be protected now."

"Yes, Father," was all Eve could say before she scampered into the cottage to be by her friend's side.

Making a Decision

"Is she able to travel?" Brin asked Cook the next morning. "I think it would be best for her to rest at least one more day. Do you feel it is that urgent? Surely the girls are safe here. You don't think Lord Albert would turn to 'Him' do you? Surely he wouldn't…."

"Lord Albert has changed," Brin interrupted. "He's not the man he once was. That wounded little girl is proof of that!"

"Did you have any idea Lord Albert had her?" Cook asked.

"I had my suspicions early on since his wife could have been nurse to the child, but then there were lots of other soldiers whose wives could have served as well. I just thought, at the time, Albert would be a good choice. He was an honorable man. Granted, he had the temper of a bull, with the strength to match, all of which was of great benefit on the battlefield. When Albert exploded, there was no foe who could stand before him. Off the battlefield, his wife always knew how to handle him; she tempered him in many ways. She was a good woman. I think we lost more people to that cursed fever than we did in the last war."

Cook shook her head. "That dread fever," she said.

Brin continued. "Ever since his wife and child died, Albert hasn't been the same man. When both our bands were summoned to council, I overheard some of his men talk of the change in him; then when I saw him, I could tell right away that something was different. His eyes were dark, empty, and spoke of great pain and sadness. I truly thought he would recover in time, but instead he has only grown worse. A short few years ago, he would have sooner died than to have caused such harm to that little girl. That assures me all the more that I must take the girls home as quickly as I can. Lord Albert is surely not in his proper mind. I'm afraid his heart has already died within, and much suffering and bitterness has bereaved him of his senses. If Lucian has discovered that Albert had the child, in his present condition, well—"

"Heaven forbid!" Cook interrupted.

"As I was praying this morning," Brin cautioned, "I felt the Lord urging me that it was time to leave, and leave soon we must."

"If it must be so, then God's will be done," Cook agreed. "He knows all things. He knows what is best, and if He says go, then you must go."

"You are right," Brin answered. "Let us prepare today while the child rests and gains what strength she is able. We shall leave tonight. We will take advantage of the protection and cover of darkness."

Brin fell silent for a moment, then, with a reflective look on his face, said, "Protecting those children, and even facing all of Lucian's army does not press upon me like the weight of truth that I am now forced to place upon that precious child. I will need more strength for that truth than this entire journey with all of its dangers to face."

And with those words Brin cast upon Cook the most helpless look she had ever seen, so that her heart was nearly ripped from her bosom. That great captain and war hero, the greatest man in the whole kingdom, aside from King Amasa himself, sat before her with tear-filled eyes and a breaking heart. Lord Brin knew full well that he was about to cross the threshold of despair and lose the one thing on earth that held his heart, the one who brought him great joy, his only daughter.

"I know you love her as your own flesh, Sir," Cook said. "Eve is a good child, and you have taught her well. She will love you no less; you shall always be her father in her heart. I feel she is strong enough; she is ready. I will pray God give you strength and courage to trust Him. You always knew this day would come."

"Yes, Cook, I know, but I just kept thinking to myself 'later,' but now that day is upon us."

Preparing for the Journey

Brin had one knight who was trusted above all others, one he had trained from his early teenage years. Johanan had proved to be a faithful and loyal friend as well as his most capable soldier despite his young age of 20 years.

Johanan was much like his father, determined in heart, focused in goals, and valiant of spirit. Johanan's father, Jedidiah, had given his life defending the king and his family in what was called "the great uprising." He died with no regrets, save one. He had fulfilled his oath as a knight, protected his lord, served his country well, and loved his God with his whole heart. His only dying regret was that he would not live to see his son grow into manhood.

As Jedidiah lay mortally wounded, he committed his son's training to the capable and caring hands of his best friend and fellow soldier, Brin. From that day forward, Brin provided for Johanan and his mother. He spent all the time he could afford with the lad and did his best to teach him not only how to be a knight but what it truly meant to be a man. To be true and honest, faithful, and honorable. He taught him the meaning of character and the power of his word, but most of all Brin taught him that a true man is one who understands he never stands taller than when he is bowed on his knees in submission to the King of All Kings.

"We are all under a greater authority," he had once told a young Johanan. "Even our King Amasa himself answers to the High King of Glory. I teach you how to fight, yet the Holy Writ says the horse is prepared against the day of battle: but safety is of the Lord. We learn and train to sharpen the skills the Lord has given to us, but in the end, everything is up to Him. Never forget, son, that He is our fortress, our strong tower, our buckler and shield, our hope, our strength, and our joy."

"But why did He have to take Father away?" the lad had asked.

"There are many things we do not know or understand. There are those who would seek to bow only to their own lusts and desires, not knowing that thus doing they are still bowing to a greater power – only it is not the power of good but of evil – and they are never satisfied. While they think they are free, they are actually brought into an even greater bondage. But we can trust our Lord Jesus, who makes us free indeed, who has a purpose and a plan that neither you nor I can perceive. His ways are not our ways. We see but the threads of this life, but our God sees the tapestry of eternity; therefore, we can trust Him." And trust Him

Johanan did, and from that time forward, he was a very different young man.

Brin rode Magi to the village of Garland that morning to inform Johanan he had a very special task for him.

"Johanan, what in the world are you doing still in bed at this late hour of the day? The sun already waxes hot and you have work to do!"

Johanan responded sleepily, "One might think that a man of your age and wisdom would have learned a thing or two about the healthful benefit of a good night's rest. Not to mention," Johanan whispered with a boyish grin, as he peeked out from under the covers, "a little known and lesser understood concept called 'beauty sleep.'"

"I didn't get to be a man of my age by sleeping my life away!"

"All right, I'm up, I'm up. What is so important that my sweet dreams must be interrupted so?" Then under his breath he added, "It's a good thing I don't need beauty sleep."

"You must come with me," Brin said, his tone serious. "We have a dangerous journey to make, and I need your help. Meet me at my cottage as soon as you can. I trust you can find your way." Then Brin was off.

And with that Johanan jumped out of bed and, as quickly as he could, dressed, set his affairs in order, gathered his things, saddled his horse, and headed for Finnley Forest. It mattered not what the task was, or where the journey was to take them, Brin had said he needed him, and that was all that mattered.

It was late afternoon when Johanan arrived at the cottage. As he rode he wondered why he had never been invited there before. He knew the general location and had no trouble finding the lane that led him there. He also wondered why Brin didn't live at his estate in the village of Garland to be closer to his men. The answer to all these questions and more became bright as brass as he rode up and saw two little girls in the cottage yard. One had long brown hair hanging in curls, the other long blond hair blowing in the breeze. Both were feeding apples to Magi, his captain's war horse.

Oh my! he thought to himself. *Is that who I think it is? Is it possible?*

Brin stepped out of the barn and watched as Johanan rode up. "I heard you coming four furlongs away, and I was in the barn! Has all my training been for naught?" Brin asked in a teasing tone that was usually reserved for family or the closest of friends.

Hardly taking his eyes from the girls Johanan replied, "Forgive me, my Captain, I had no idea.... I mean, I wasn't expecting.... Uh...." And suddenly gathering his wits he added, "Captain, when do we leave?"

"Tonight," Brin answered, "under cover of darkness."

DIRECTION

"Ladies, I'd like you to meet Johanan. Johanan, I'd like to introduce to you Eve and Dawn."

Eve gave a small curtsey and said, "A pleasure, Sir." Dawn tried to hide behind her friend.

Johanan dismounted and said, "I am at your service, my lady," and gave a bow. Then stepping round to the side of Eve, he got a good look at Dawn, saw the marks of abuse, and his heart sank. Facing her he bowed on one knee and smiled his sweet boyish smile and said, "And I am at your service as well, my lady." There was something so reassuring in the way he said it that made Dawn gather the courage to look into that handsome smiling face. When she did so, she determined she need not fear him after all, so she tried to do as her friend had done and curtsey, without the slightest idea how her friend had done it and wound up doing sort of a hop and bow. Stifling a chuckle, Johanan said, "Very nicely done, my lady."

"Children," Brin said, "if you feed all our apples to Magi now, we won't have any for our journey. Go inside and help Cook with dinner. Please inform her that we have a guest who will be staying."

"Yes, Father," Eve replied. "Come on, Dawn." They scampered into the kitchen.

"Father?" Johanan asked, and without waiting for an answer said, "You've had one of the children? This whole time? I never knew!"

"You weren't supposed to know," Brin answered.

"What of the younger one? Where has she been, and most importantly, who has mistreated her so? Who would do such a thing?"

"Lord Albert," Brin said.

"Lord Albert? Tell me nay! How could that be? How could he have been given one of the children?"

"He wasn't always the hard man that you know today. He was once a good and honorable man, before he lost his wife and daughter to the fever."

"I see. Where is he now?"

"I know not. I only know that we must leave tonight. I shall tell you all I know as we travel. For now, let us see whether Cook has dinner ready."

"Amen to that, my Captain. I'm starving!"

"You are always starving!"

"Tis true, Sir," Johanan answered laughing. "Tis true."

Inside Cook had a wonderful meal prepared, and while they ate, the men talked of the best route to take.

"It boils down to which way is safest for the girls," Brin said. "The quickest way is in the open along the king's highway, but the longer way through Wylderland provides plenty of cover."

"Yes, but it also provides plenty of other things. They don't call it Wylderland for naught! Lucian himself wouldn't dare venture into those woods."

"Precisely," answered Brin. "I don't think Lucian would venture that way."

"But, Captain, you know the stories of that place," Johanan declared. "The woods are so thick even the light of the sun does not penetrate. It's full of strange creatures, and people who venture there are never to be seen again."

"Well, if that's so," Brin said, raising an eyebrow, "then where do the stories come from? If no one ever came out to tell the tale, then there would be no story."

Johanan blushed. "I never thought of it that way, I guess."

"Don't tell me that you who does not flinch at battle, you whom I've seen take on ten men single-handed, you who charges in first and leaves last, are afraid of a little patch of woods?"

"Of course not," Johanan said confidently, chin raised. "I was just thinking of the children, that's all."

"Certainly," Brin replied as he tried to hold in his smile. At that, Dawn came to Johanan's side and said so soft and tenderly, "It will be all right, I walk in the woods at night alone all the time. I will help you if you like."

"It would be an honor, my lady. If you would accompany me, it would be most helpful."

"That settles it, then," Brin announced. "We ride northeast to Wylderland."

Eve spoke up and said, "But, Father, you have yet to tell us where we are going. I've never even been to the village before, and now you talk of a great journey through the dangers of Wylderland. I don't understand."

"You will understand it all in time, my daughter, in time."

The Adventure Begins

Supper eaten, plans made, provisions packed, and everything ready, Cook took Eve aside and said, "Eve, my dear, I want you to know that whatever happens, you are as precious to me as if you were my own child. Remember all that I have taught you. You must needs take care of your father for me now."

"I will take good care of him," Eve replied. "I promise."

"I know you will. Be strong and take courage. Never forget how much I love you."

"But I will see you again soon, won't I?" Eve said as a tear trickled down her cheek.

"I dearly hope so, my child."

"It is time," Brin said. "We must go."

Cook gave Eve one last hug and, holding back her own tears, whispered, "The Blood of Christ binds us into a more sure family than that of mortal man. I love you," and then kissed her on her head.

"And I love you, Cook," Eve managed to whisper back.

As the sun was setting and the moon arose, off they went. It was a pleasant night with a clear sky when suddenly, as if out of everywhere, the darkness sparkled with thousands of twinkling lights. Stars! But Eve hardly noticed. Her head was swimming with thoughts and confusion and fears. *What did it all mean? What was happening? Where were they going? Why did Cook talk as if she was never coming home? What wouldn't her father tell her?*

Dawn spoke and drew Eve away from her dark thoughts. "Eve! Look at the sky! Is it not beautiful? Does it not look like thousands of diamonds sparkling? I think it must be God's crown; since He is everywhere, He would have a simply enormous one!"

Eve looked up and for the first time began to notice the beautiful night surrounding them. Then she realized how safe she felt sitting astride Magi behind her strong father. She slipped her arms around his waist and buried her head into his back and wept softly.

"Everything will be all right," he assured her. "Don't worry, my daughter." So Eve plucked up her courage, straightened, and tried to enjoy the ride while Brin's heart fell within as he realized the time had come that he would no longer be able to call his diamond "my daughter."

They rode side by side for some time quietly picking their path. Then coming to a stream, they dismounted to give the horses a rest and a drink.

"Let's walk a bit, shall we?" Brin said. And so they traveled that night, riding a while and walking a while. After some time it became apparent that Dawn had spent all her strength, although she uttered not a word.

Johanan said, "My lady, come, I will carry you." A weak smile crossed her face as she held out her arms to him. Although the swelling had gone and the bruises were healing, she was still very weak. Johanan noticed that she hardly had the strength to hold on to him as he carried her, and his heart melted afresh for the tender child he now carried in his arms.

The sunrise found Dawn asleep in the saddle leaning against Johanan who held her securely with one arm. They traveled a few more hours until they found a suitable spot to camp and sleep for the remainder of the day. The men bedded the children down in a pleasant shaded cove.

"Once we reach Wylderland, we shall travel by day," Brin whispered.

"It matters not if we travel by day or night in that cursed place," Johanan replied. "It is always dark, they say."

"There shall be a little light. You will see. When it is very dark, a little light makes a big difference. Now go, take some rest; I will take the first watch."

A New Beginning

lbert woke stiff and sore lying on the ground against the base of a huge tree. He was dazed, confused, and utterly disoriented. "How in the world did I get here?" He had ridden hard through the night, blinded by his emotion, and had paid no heed to direction or time as he spurred his horse forward. He vaguely remembered crossing a stream, or maybe it was a river. He didn't know or care. He remembered something about water splashing around him. Or had the water come from his own eyes?

Where was he and how long had he lain there? Everything seemed a blur. Then as he looked down, he saw little patches of dried blood on his hands and shirt. Suddenly, he heard a noise and jumped to his feet only to find that it was his horse tearing up the grass just a few feet away. Then the floodgate opened, and the memory of the night before and how he had exploded on little Dawn came rushing in on him. He felt like one who suddenly remembers a horrible nightmare. Only Albert knew it was no dream, but very real.

"What have I done? Oh my! What have I done? How could I have done such a thing? Oh my soul! What have I done?" Albert yelled as he fell to his knees crying, sobbing, half screaming, the weight of reality more than he could bear. Finally, every ounce of his strength gave way and he fell to his face in the grass wailing. Then he began to pray aloud. "Oh my God in heaven, is there forgiveness for me? Is there forgiveness for me? Can you forgive one so wicked and vile? I am so sorry! In my pain I have hurt the only person I have left in this world. I have been so blinded by my sorrow and bitterness. I didn't mean to take it all out on the child, truly I didn't. It's not her fault! It's mine!"

As a man who has been crazed finally awakes to his senses, Albert awoke. His eyes were opened for the very first time since the death of his wife and child, and he hated what he saw.

God, in His mercy, shut the mouth of his own flesh and the voices of devils, and allowed Albert for the very first time in his life to see and hear clearly. Not with the eyes of men or of angels, but as God sees. That is why Albert loathed what he saw with a vehement hatred. He could see himself as God saw him and, oh, what a wretched miserable sight it was.

Albert had gone to church all of his life before his wife and child passed a few years earlier. He had been a decent, moral man, for the most part, at least as good as the next, or so he thought. But in actuality, he had never taken God or His word very seriously – at least not seriously enough to allow it to change his life or anything like that, and certainly not seriously enough to bow his proud neck to the yoke of Christ. But this day something was profoundly different. This day was like none other Albert had ever known. God in His providence had chosen this day, a day of tumult and trouble, to break the back of pride in the vilest of sinners.

Until this very moment Albert could easily recognize all the hurt and injustice ever imposed upon him, yet he could never see his own shortcomings. Every trouble, every miserable circumstance, and every unfortunate event from time and eternity seemed to Albert a fit excuse to lash out violently at everyone and everything. But this day, Albert could see his greatest enemy, his most dangerous foe, and, to his great surprise, it was his own sinful heart.

Albert could also see something else, Christ Jesus, for who He really was. So much more than a babe in a manger, more than just a man his mother's Bible talked about, and so much more than he had ever imagined. He was Lord, and Albert had never bowed before His majesty. But He was also Redeemer, Savior, and Friend of sinners.

With this new awakening, Albert bowed his head, opened his repentant heart, and with a child-like faith prayed as he had never prayed before.

For a long time, Albert lay on his face crying out to God, and the God of all Glory, whose mercy is from everlasting to everlasting, the One who had awakened him, heard this sinner's prayer. When forgiveness came, it was as if the weight of the entire world had been lifted from his shoulders. Then suddenly, for the first time in three long years, he heard himself chuckle. *Peace!* Wonderful peace flooded his heart.

He had been forgiven! Dark had been his days, but now he was in the light – glorious light – and it made him want to laugh and cry all at once.

"I must go home. I have to tell Dawn how sorry I am that I have been such a terrible man, but now she has a new father. I just pray God will put it in her heart to forgive me. Maybe we could start all over. I could beg the king leave for a short while so as to make amends. Dear Father," Albert prayed, "as You have forgiven me, please allow the child to grant me one more chance at being a real father. I beg You, please, please let her forgive me."

Albert struggled to his feet and found the saddle where he had thrown it off sometime that morning and saddled his horse once again. Except this time he didn't climb on for he could see the toll he had taken on his poor horse with his hard driving. "It's going to be all right, ol' boy. I'm sorry I rode you so hard last night. I haven't taken very good care of you either, have I? I'm happy to say you have a new master now, and I will do my best to take better care of you. What do you say to this – we both walk?" he asked as he gently patted the horse's side. Then a strange thing happened. His horse looked him square in the eyes as if to say, "It's all right. I forgive you." So with fresh tears running down his face Albert did something else he hadn't done in a very long time. He hugged the neck of his horse and his horse nuzzled him in return.

"Let's head home, shall we?" But it didn't take long for Albert to realize he didn't know exactly where home was. "Well, old friend, this might be easier said than done. I wasn't exactly thinking straight as we rode last night, was

I? Do you have any idea where we are? I'm afraid I have no recollection of this place. There is nothing to be done but to track our own trail as we did Lucian to the outer edge of the kingdom."

It took almost an hour for Albert to find the direction they had traveled the previous night because his horse being free to roam and graze at will had left quite a maze of hoof prints. Eventually Albert spotted the trail and by the deep-set hoof marks was confident that the horse was carrying his load at that point. He could then pick up the traces of his trek.

"This shall be slow going, old friend," Albert said to his horse, "but with God's help, everything will come out right in the end."

As they walked, following their own trail, Albert prayed for Dawn, that she would be all right, that God would look after her and care for her until he could make it home. He prayed over and over again for her to find it in her heart to forgive him. So on they walked.

It took the better part of two full days to finally reach the village of Blain, which was the town nearest to his humble home in Finnley Forest, but they were good days. Albert had never known that fellowship with God could be so real, and the feeling was more wonderful than words could describe. As he walked through the village leading his horse, a knot formed in the pit of his stomach at the thought of facing Dawn. He was happy and scared all at the same time.

As he was thinking on these things, he began to notice something most peculiar. As he ambled along through the village, people began to scurry away. When they spotted him about to pass by, they would duck behind a garden wall, suddenly spiral down some other lane, or turn round and head in another direction. He had never noticed people hiding from him before. But their behavior made clear the fact that most common villagers had learned to avoid him, likely because they branded him an ill-tempered blighter long ago. Lord Albert had simply never cared enough to notice before.

He started calling out as he went, "Good afternoon," "Fine day," "The Lord bless you," and as he did folks would simply stare at him with eyes and mouths wide open. Others who found their voice would reply, "Uh, uh, good day to you, Lord Albert." It made him smile all the more, and Albert was much amused at his newfound oddity. Oh, if they only knew how different he really was.

As the sun was setting and the moon arose, Albert stood in the open doorway of his empty little hovel. His joy turned quickly to sorrow, and tears streamed freely down his tired and lonely face. The shack was dark and painfully silent. His little girl was gone.

FINDING THEIR PLACE

As Brin, Johanan, and the two girls traveled toward Wylderland and parts beyond, a new transformation began to take shape, as each member of the company found her or his proper place.

Eve quickly assumed the role of mother to the group, wanting to keep the promise she had made to Cook to look after her father. It came to her quite naturally. Cook had taught her well, and she enjoyed cooking and what little cleaning could be done while they traveled and camped.

As their supplies dwindled, Johanan would hunt small game to roast over the fire, and Eve kept her eye open for fruits, wild berries, and any nuts that could be found along the way. Eve was very happy spending time with her father during these days. How proud she was to show him she could mend the fire, roast the meat (after Johanan had skinned and cleaned it, of course), and even tend to the horses. Yes, Eve had found her lot in life. She also took special care of her secret sister Dawn, making sure she ate plenty and always carrying more of the load when they would have to fetch water or wood for the fire. As the days wore on her friend began to show the ill effects of traveling, and Eve kept a watchful eye on her. They grew even closer, though both girls had believed that was not possible.

Dawn had no trouble finding her role as encourager of the group. Weak and frail as she was, she never complained, but faced each task head on and gave it her all. With a meek and humble spirit, she always seemed to have the right word at the right time. With childish innocence and wisdom beyond her years, Dawn touched the hearts of everyone in the group.

Hand in hand the girls relied on each other, as together they would climb the steep hills, jump over the narrow gullies, and cross the swollen streams, while the men took much care to lead the horses and choose the best and safest path for them all.

Dawn was always busy pointing out the wonders of creation – a pretty bird, beautiful wildflowers, or colorful rocks. If she wasn't looking for some animal track, she was waiting for the clouds to form an exciting new shape.

She had the innocent child-like ability to live every moment to its fullest. She was enjoying herself immensely. When Eve asked her about it, she said she had always dreamt of being off on some grand adventure instead of being a prisoner in her home. This trip was something she could have only dreamed of, and now it was real. She wanted to enjoy every minute of it.

After that talk Eve stopped worrying about the where's and the why's and just enjoyed the time she had with her new family group. Yes, Dawn was definitely the encourager.

Johanan became the protector. He grew especially fond of Dawn. He would carry her when her strength would fail, yet he always found a good reason so as not to embarrass the child. He wondered how such a small frame could contain so much courage and determination. They formed a special bond on the basis of trust and shared many talks during the times he carried her.

As the days passed, Brin grew somber and talked less and less. He seemed content to watch the girls and listen to them as they played such games as they could while traveling. He marveled how even though the girls had only been together a short time, they instinctively acted like sisters. Eve was always trying to mother Dawn, and Dawn would try to do everything Eve did.

Brin knew he needed to tell them, but he just couldn't bring himself to do it. Every day he would say, "Tomorrow, I shall tell them tomorrow." Yet when tomorrow came, something always seemed to stand in the way. The time somehow never felt right. So after getting the girls settled in for a rest one day, Brin crept away to be alone with his Lord. "Father, I don't understand. I believe You told me to take the girls home, and I believe we are taking the route You set down for us. But, I'm confused. Am I to tell the girls now? Did I miss Your will by not telling them sooner? Or has the pain in my heart and the weakness of my own flesh robbed me of the courage to do what I must? Yes, Lord, I do know Your grace is sufficient, and you will give it when it is needed. Yes, Lord, I know time means nothing to You, but timing is everything. Thank You, Lord. I understand. Give me the grace and strength I need when the time is right. You possess all wisdom and power. Protect us as we travel, and Your will be done. Amen."

Brin could rest again with peace in his heart. His God had everything in hand. The time had simply not been right.

Venturing into the Unknown

"And you're sure you want to go in there?" asked Johanan as the tiny band stood at the border of the forest they called "Wylderland."

"Yes," Brin replied. "I believe in my heart this is the path the Lord has chosen for us. And if it truly is God's path we are traveling, then He will certainly watch over us, and all shall be well."

"If you say so," answered Johanan. "You are the Captain."

"I say so." And with that Brin led a trembling company, with the exception of Dawn, into the dreaded forest.

"One would never know it is late morning," remarked Johanan as they walked.

"But there is light," Brin reminded him. "It isn't completely dark, just as I said."

Dawn spoke up and said, "I think it is a sad forest – not an evil place, just a sad place."

"I believe you are right," answered Eve. "But still, something seems amiss. It feels as if the trees have eyes and are watching us."

Everyone was on edge with their eyes darting this way and that and jumping at every sound. They were all nervous, everyone except Dawn. She seemed strangely at ease and content, enjoying the quiet and marveling at all the new scenes around her.

Johanan noticed the peaceful look on her face and said, "My lady, may I ask you a question?"

"Certainly," she replied.

"Are you not afraid?"

"Of this forest, you mean?"

"Yes, of this place?"

"No, not at all. It holds a strange and wonderful beauty. Everything is calm and in order without a lot of outside influence messing it up. It is like everything is in its place fulfilling its purpose. If you know what I mean."

"Maybe I do understand, a little," Johanan answered, in the throes of his own wonder.

"I just hope," she started to continue, then cut her words short.

"You hope *what*, my lady?"

"I hope to fulfill my purpose and to know what it is," she answered.

"What are you speaking of?"

"I am not long for this world," she replied matter-of-factly.

"Why would you say such a thing?"

"Because I just know, but you mustn't tell Eve. She would just worry. Promise me you won't tell Eve until the time comes!"

"I am sure you are mistaken," Johanan replied, wondering where the child could have arrived at such a conclusion. "Yet rest assured, your secret is safe with me." He knew traveling had taken its toll on her, and yes, she was very frail, but there was nothing wrong that a few days of rest and plenty to eat wouldn't take care of when they reached their destination.

Dawn interrupted his thoughts and said, "May I ask you a question?"

"Certainly, my lady, you may ask me anything."

"What is it that you are so fearful of?"

"Well," he began slowly, not quite sure how to soften his answer, "there are stories of a danger that lurks in these woods of unknown proportions. People have simply disappeared without a trace. Others say some strange animal lives here – part bear and part man – and reigns as king of this forest. His eyes see all his borders and he knows when strangers trespass his lands. Few, if any, are allowed safe passage, and all others meet some horrible fate."

Dawn shook her head. "I do not think we have anything to fear. In fact I feel we are all very safe."

"I hope you are right, my lady. I hope you are right."

They then traveled on in silence, following what looked to be a very old path, when suddenly Dawn cried out, "Look at that!" Her sharp eyes had spotted a mark high in a nearby tree. It appeared to be three huge scratches, deep and wide, as if made by giant talons.

"What on earth could have made such marks?" Johanan asked. "It's higher than any animal, and no human could reach that height, even standing atop his horse, and once more they go across the tree, not down it!" Johanan was speaking as his mind quickly sifted through all the forest stories he could recall.

Brin answered, wanting to keep the children calm. "Maybe some strange new bird looking for a meal under the bark of the tree."

"No bird made those marks. They are definitely animal-like scratches. I warned you there are dangerous creatures in these woods," Johanan finished.

"Thank you for all your help in not alarming the children," Brin said in a sarcastic tone as he gave Johanan a sideways look. "I can always count on you." Then he yielded. "I see you are right; swords to the ready. Children, hold on tight to our backs. Dawn, keep a keen watch for more signs in the trees." Brin knew, child as she was, Dawn had better eyes than his best scout. "Quietly now," he said as they moved forward. Dawn grabbed hold of the back of Johanan's belt and held on tight. He held his sword in one hand and the reins in the other.

As they rode Dawn spotted more signs, always very high in a tree and always three marks deep and wide crossways. They were undoubtedly in someone or some thing's domain, and they knew it. Eve was terrified and tried hard not to shake as she gripped the back of Brin's belt until her knuckles were white and her palms red. They traveled on.

Even though it was still early, the group noticed they were beginning to lose what little daylight they had.

"We must find a suitable place to camp for the night," Brin said, breaking the silence. "Darkness will soon be upon us."

"Yes, it is coming on fast," replied Johanan. They soon came upon a huge tree with enormous reaching roots that they could all snuggle against, as if the tree was protecting them in an embrace.

"This looks good," Brin remarked.

Johanan grabbed his quiver and bow from his pack. "Children, if you will see to a fire, I shall venture out with what light is left and maybe the Good Lord will provide us with some fresh meat for dinner."

"Stay within sight," Brin added. "There are lots of dry branches for the fire close at hand."

"Yes, Father," Eve replied. The children had no trouble finding plenty of fuel and getting a nice fire going while Brin tended the horses and saddles and packs. They had all begun to relax in the warmth and comfort of the campfire when suddenly the pre-dusk calm was shattered by a bloodcurdling scream.

An Unexpected Visitor

"Stay here!" Brin shouted to the girls as he drew his sword and ran off in the direction of Johanan's cry. The two girls looked at each other and without a word took off following Brin. Not far ahead they found Johanan and Brin standing shoulder to shoulder looking straight ahead.

"What is it, Father?" Eve asked as they came up beside them. Before he could answer she saw for herself: Bones, lots of bones, hanging from several branches of the trees, and many other trees had the same curious markings they had seen earlier.

Then Eve saw the sign, written in scratch-like letters: "Enterers beware; ye have entered the realm of the Bear King. Return or be dispatched."

"What does that mean?" asked Dawn. "Return or be dispatched?"

"It means someone wants us to go away," answered Brin. Then he turned to Johanan and asked, "What on earth was the scream all about?"

"Well," he began slowly, "I was following what looked to be a game trail, when I thought I heard a fallow deer grunting in the laurel up ahead. I figured a nice roast of venison would make a wonderful dinner for the children. I found some tracks, took off following them, and I guess I had my head down watching the trail instead of looking ahead of me. When I rose up to peer into the bushes, I found myself surrounded by a maze of these decrepit old bones, hitting me right in the face. Maybe I was just a little on edge. Sorry."

Brin snickered and said, "Yea, maybe a little on edge. This is all just meant to scare people away, and we are not going anywhere except back to camp. Come on. We shall eat from our packs tonight. Brin turned and looked at the girls standing behind him. "I thought I told you children to stay at camp?" he said.

"Well," Eve started to say, stuttering as she went on, "well, uh, you see, uh, we both just felt as if we should follow you, didn't we, Dawn?"

"Yes, Sir, we did."

"All right, I shall let it pass this time, but from now on I expect the both of you to obey my word, understand?"

"Yes, Father," Eve replied.

"Yes, Sir," Dawn added.

Then Brin let out a chuckle to himself and elbowed Johanan as they walked and said, "The great Johanan, squealing like a girl, what would the men say?" Then he laughed again.

In the most dignified tone he could muster Johanan said, "Seeing as how the men are not here, and they shall not be told, then I shall not worry my head about it."

"All right, all right, far be it from me to repeat the tale, but you know how children are prone to talk. I do admit there is something about this place that unnerves the soul. I might have done the same in your position – squeal like a girl, that is. Naw, I take that back."

The girls tried to hold in their laughter as they followed behind the men, but at last they couldn't contain themselves any longer and together burst out laughing. The whole company was laughing as they stepped into the circle of light that encompassed their camp. Their laughter came to an abrupt end as the figure of a man stepped out from the shadows behind the mammoth tree into the blazing firelight. Brin and Johanan quick as a flash drew their swords as Dawn shouted, "Father!" and cowered behind Johanan.

Brin spoke in a firm tone, "Lord Albert."

Albert responded, "Lord Brin."

"What do you want?" Brin questioned.

"I want to talk to Dawn."

A torrent of rage swept through Johanan as he gripped his sword tightly in one hand and sheltered Dawn behind himself with the other. "Haven't you caused enough pain and damage to this child?" Then Johanan braced himself for the fight that was surely about to come.

But there was no quarrel whatsoever. Albert stood motionless and humbled, then with tear-filled eyes answered softly, "Far too much pain."

It was soon plain to see swords were not needed here, for Albert was a broken man. Even though they put their swords away, Johanan still kept Dawn behind him as if to shield her from some unforeseen danger.

"That is why I have come all this way," continued Albert. "I don't know where to start, but I have come to ask Dawn if she can find it in her heart to forgive me. I had to tell her that God has changed me; that I am not the same man who hurt her. God has forgiven me, and although I know I don't deserve it, I ask that she find it in her heart to forgive me also."

With that Dawn peaked around the side of Johanan and saw the look in his eyes. It was a different look, a new look. For the first time in a very long time, she saw love in his face instead of anger.

"Oh, Father!" she cried as she pushed Johanan aside and bolted toward Albert with open arms.

He caught her up and held her tight, crying, "I'm so sorry. I'm so sorry. Please forgive me. I never meant to hurt you."

"I forgive you, Father. I forgive you," Dawn managed to get out, and she cried as though her heart would break. Yet in between sobs they could hear a laugh, and everyone knew she was crying for joy. They held on to each other for the longest time, and when Dawn finally spoke she said, "I only want you to love me, Father."

"Oh, my darling, I do love you. Though I didn't show it, I have always loved you!" As the hugs gave way, Albert looked at Brin and said, "Lord Brin, you are a good man. Can you also find it in your heart to forgive me?"

"Of course," Brin said. "If God has forgiven you, then who am I not to do likewise? But, what shall I forgive you for? You have wronged the child, not me."

Albert answered, "For forcing you to take this journey. You are taking the children home. Am I correct?"

"Yes," Brin answered.

Eve interrupted. "Home, what are you talking about, Father. We left home days ago?"

Looking Eve in the eyes, he answered, "It is time, my child; I shall now do my best to answer all of your many questions though it will no doubt pain me very much."

Seeing the sadness in her father's face, Eve suddenly became sick to her stomach and said, "I don't think I want to know now."

"The time has come, my darling. You must know the truth."

DEEP SECRETS REVEALED

As the company sat around the campfire, Brin began the long and difficult task of explaining to the girls the stunning truth that lay beneath their shrouded past. He told them all about how Lucian had been the king's most trusted advisor and outwardly the king's best friend until Lucian decided that he should be king. "He wanted all the reverence, authority, and everything else that came with being king, but Lucian had no legitimate claim to the throne. He had not the right bloodline or even the right heart to reign over such a kingdom as Peacehaven. He became so envious and jealous of King Amasa that he finally convinced himself that he truly did deserve to rule the kingdom."

Brin continued. "He then began to plot against the king. He drew men of the baser sort to his side, working just as Absalom did. With the subtlety of a serpent, Lucian stole the hearts of men and turned their affections and loyalty away from the true king and steered them toward himself. Those who were disgruntled or imagined the king had in some way wronged them were easy prey. Lucian has a cunning silver tongue and can beguile even the best of hearts if they are not on their guard. Others were simply bought with a price."

"He secretly raised an army and was almost ready to put his plan of revolt into action when divine providence allowed Johanan's father, Jedidiah, to overhear this evil plot. Jedidiah came to me straightway and reported all that he had heard and, working together, we gathered all the proof necessary to convince King Amasa of Lucian's treason and inform him of the plot to overthrow the kingdom. At first the king didn't want to believe it. But then the Lord opened his heart, and the words we spoke rang true. It answered many questions that had troubled the king's heart. He could then see clearly how all the pieces fit together with Lucian's behavior: the long, frequent absences from court; the strange, rough-looking men coming and going from the castle late at night; and, finally, the accounting errors discovered in the king's treasury."

"Heretofore, Lucian had dismissed the king's concerns so easily. He always had a quick answer to every question. Most telling, though, was that King Amasa had detected a change in Lucian himself. He couldn't quite put his finger on it, yet deep down he knew something had changed in his old friend. The king on occasion had even tried to ask him if something was wrong, but Lucian's tongue could be sweet as honey and more slippery than butter. Oh, how it grieved the king's heart to be betrayed by one so close, trusted, and loved."

"At last the king called him forward and pressed the matter against him. Everything had been made manifest. Lucian at first tried to smooth talk his way out of it, but when he saw that the king was no longer going to be fooled, he became dark and poisonous like the serpent he really is."

"'You are weak, my old friend,' Lucian told him, through clenched teeth. 'The success of your rule is due to me and my council. You would not be what you are today had it not been for me!'"

"King Amasa said, 'No, you are wrong; would you remove Almighty God from His throne as well? The success of my father's house is because the Lord God of Heaven in His sovereign will hath ordained it so. *Not by might, nor by power, but by My Spirit saith the Lord of hosts.* Not one blessing that has befallen me is by the will of man, and by all means, not by the work of an unfaithful councillor such as yourself.'"

"Lucian sneered. 'You seek proof? I shall give you a bitter example. That throne is rightfully mine!' And with cursing and threats Lucian shouted aloud, 'Arise men, now is the time! FIGHT!'"

"The treachery proved great, and many of the king's own guard fell away and began a violent assault on those faithful to the king. It was a distressing and costly battle, but when the fray at last ended, evil had been defeated. Johanan's father fell mortally wounded that day defending the king's own person. Lucian stood back, far from harm's way and looked on like the coward he truly is. Even though his treasonous sedition was worthy of death, King Amasa sought to show great mercy and to honor all the good that had once existed in Lucian. Thus the king made a proclamation that, in lieu of execution, Lucian be banished forthwith from the kingdom."

"But as Lucian was being led away, he shouted, 'This day you seek to strip me of everything I hold dear, but there will come a day when I shall take your most precious possession from you. And, my friend, this time I speak not of your throne. I shall take something more precious, yes, *much* more precious.'"

"'Get him out of here before I change my mind!' King Amasa shouted. Had the king been a lesser man he may have had Lucian's head that day, but his word was his bond. So with that, Lucian was forever exiled from the kingdom."

"As the days passed, King Amasa grew more and more uneasy. In his heart he understood perfectly the intent of Lucian's vulgar threats. There was little doubt concerning the earthly thing most precious to his royal highness, his two beloved daughters, the apples of his eyes. Lucian knew his children were worth more to him than a dozen thrones or kingdoms. And so now all the king's thoughts were bent on how to protect the children."

"Then word came that many men had left the kingdom and gathered themselves to Lucian. This new army sealed Lucian's fate. 'I had thought to show him mercy, but he has put mercy from him. I have no choice but to issue a warrant for his arrest. Until he is captured, to ensure the safety of my beloved daughters, they shall be divided and entrusted to the care of guardians. This guardianship will provide the children protection, anonymity, and relative comfort until this present distress shall be resolved. They shall be able to carry on, as much as can be, a normal life, free from fear. Those who care for the children shall be properly rewarded but in no wise, under any condition, shall they disclose the nature of the matter to anyone. The guardians shall treat the children as their own until the day that Lucian is captured, at which time they can safely return home. In the event that the children are somehow discovered, the guardians must immediately seek the protection of the castle and the king's guard. There are no words in the tongues of men or angels to describe how deeply the queen and I are grieved by this sudden separation from our beloved daughters, but their safety compels us to do what must be done. I have placed their wellbeing into the Lord's hands, for there and only there are they truly safe.'"

Brin turned to Eve. "So, Eve—"

Eve cut him off. "I am the eldest daughter of King Amasa."

"Yes, it is true. You were the eldest and already weaned and, therefore, given to me to protect. I hired Cook, and together we became a family, and the two of us have cared for you these eight years."

Albert turned to speak to Dawn, who by this time was a bit taken back, yet all ears and eager to listen. "You, Dawn, were just an infant when you came to us. My wife had recently given birth and was thus able to nurse you alongside our own baby girl. I had never seen her so happy. She loved you just as much as if she had given birth to you herself. Those were the happiest few years of our life. Everyday was fresh and new, full of joy and wonder. Then the fever came and took them both away, and the two of us were left all alone.

I was so vexed and confused beyond mortal understanding. I was full of wrath and rage that finally everything in me or about me was utterly consumed by a loathsome bitterness. And though naught of this was your doing, somehow you bore much of the blame. I am truly sorry. So grieved was I over what had been taken from me that I abandoned the one small treasure that had been given me." Once again Albert began to weep softly.

The girls sat stunned, speechless, staring into the firelight. Eve's mind was racing a million leagues a minute and in a thousand different directions. Then suddenly, an old familiar memory came to her. She had always had in her mind the image of a huge room, lavishly furnished, and another image of a tall man, a bit heavy with curly brown hair, but she could never quite remember his face. When she had thought on these memories, it was as if she was trying to recall some dream. In fact, she had determined that the images must surely have been from a dream. Now she knew those images in her mind came from no dream but were in fact all she could recall from her previous life. After a long silence, she looked at Brin and said, "My real father has curly brown hair like mine, doesn't he?"

Sadly, he nodded. "Yes, he does. How did you know?"

"Just an image I've carried around in my head, but I thought it was from a dream."

Suddenly Eve and Dawn looked at each other and together blurted out at once, "What of our mother?"

Albert spoke up and said, "Dawn, you are the very picture of your mother – petite, long blond hair, and very beautiful. Your mother loved you both very much, and it devastated her to lose you. She also wished you both to be safe and happy above her own desires. She was very sad for a long time, hoping each day might be the day Lucian was arrested and her precious daughters could come home. Then the plague came, and she devoted her whole heart and a good bit of the royal treasury to care for orphans left by the fever, until at last the fever took her as well. She was a wonderful woman who gave her life in the service of others. I think in her heart she was caring for the two of you as she tended those orphans."

What a melancholy group it was, sitting around the campfire that night. Silence held them captive, suspended in time, until the fire died down to a pile of smoldering embers. Each one was engulfed in his or her own thoughts. Johanan thought of his brave father dying for the king and of how he wanted to live up to the legacy and honor his father's name. Albert thought of his lost wife and child; Brin grieved for the child he was about to lose; and the children sat bewildered. They had lost family, gained family, and lost family again all in a few moments' time. It was far too much for two so young to comprehend.

Finally Dawn, the encourager, spoke and brought a welcome end to the silence. "Hey, Eve, we really are sisters! Honest and for true real sisters!"

"Yes, I guess we are," Eve responded, as she slowly turned to look at Dawn. "We truly are Secret Sisters! How wonderful!"

And with that the girls grabbed each other giggling and laughing. Their mirth lifted the mood for everyone.

Brin continued. "So now you know everything, except about your names. Eve, you were born as the sun was setting in the glow of the evening, and Dawn, you were born with the rising of the sun and the breaking of the dawn. While you are different as night and day, you have found the common bond that links you together as a chain. You are sisters." With that the girls hugged and laughed even harder.

Albert spoke up and said, "I don't know how you knew, but you were wise to head for the castle with the children. Lucian's treachery runs deeper than you know. I know not how, but he has indeed discovered that I am the guardian of Dawn. We received reports that Lucian was spotted with some bandits at the western most edge of the kingdom, and my band and I went to investigate. Lucian was there all right; late one night, while I was walking alone, he called to me from among the trees. I could never pinpoint where he was; his voice kept changing directions. He told me...." His voice faded.

"He told you *what?*" Brin asked.

"He told me he knew whom I kept and said all he wanted was to care for the child to prove his innocence. He spoke as if he could read my mind. How smooth his words were. I refused, but was so shaken we headed home at first light the next day."

"I see," said Brin, understanding fully now what had happened.

"I am truly sorry." Albert added, "I never meant to hurt anyone. I returned home, and when Dawn wasn't there, I feared Lucian had taken her already. She finally came home, and I exploded." Albert then recounted how he rode hard all that night blinded by his emotions and how God had used the whole episode to open his eyes and bring him to a place of repentance. Albert glowed as he told how God had so tenderly come to him the next day and offered him faith and forgiveness, which he gladly accepted. He then told of his long walk home only to find Dawn missing and how he had tracked them to Brin's cottage. He explained everything to Cook who rejoiced with him. She told him of Dawn's condition and how Brin and Johanan had planned to travel through Wylderland to take the children home. "So I tracked you here, but I must say, Johanan, that scream of yours gave me quite a start." He chuckled, then added, "By the way, what in the world could all these strange signs that I've seen along the way mean?"

"You mean the three sideways scratches high on the trees?" Brin asked.

"Yes. I can't think of any creature that could have made such marks."

"The same creature that hung the bones I stuck my face into," said Johanan sheepishly. Then he added, "I have a question growing in my mind. If Lucian discovered you had Dawn, then why would he have not just taken her while you were away?"

"I've wondered the same thing," Albert admitted.

Brin, thinking out loud more than anything, said, "Perhaps he came while she was off playing deep in the woods, or maybe he hadn't figured out the hiding place of the other child and had hoped you would lead him to her. Maybe one wasn't enough; he had to have both," The men exchanged knowing glances, aware that Brin had struck on the truth.

"Then I have failed you all," Albert said.

"No, no, not yet," Brin continued. "The Lord led us this way. Nothing surprises Him. He knew you would follow and find us. He knows if Lucian followed you. The Lord knows what He is doing, for we know that all things work together for good to them that love God, to them who are the called according to His purpose. Have we not sacrificed our lives, spending countless hours away from home, tracking this snake only to have him slither away in the end? No, my friends. This is the Lord's doing. He is bringing all things together for good. Be of good cheer. If God be for us, who could be against us? Albert, you are tired. Get some rest. We shall need you ready and able to fight. Children, you also need to be in bed. Johanan, I shall take the first watch. You could use a bit of rest, after your frightful encounter." Brin then bellowed a hearty laugh. He felt lighter than he had in years. The burden he had carried for so long had finally been lifted, and he knew in his spirit that God was in control.

Watchers in the Night

"Sir Marcus, are we simply going to allow this group to pass through? We've never allowed anyone to travel past the hanging bones before, or at least the few who were bold enough to try. This group means to go through!" came the voice from among the trees.

"Peace, Artemas. I know the leader of this company. He is a good man, and I believe I know his errand. If my eyes are not deceived, those are the children of King Amasa and the late Queen Grace of the kingdom of Peacehaven to the north and west of us. The oldest child is the living picture of the King himself. It seems as if they are taking the children to the castle by way of this forest."

"But why? That would be several days journey through rough terrain, a great distance out of their way, when they could travel the King's highway?"

"Why, indeed?" came the answer. "Allow them to pass unharmed; we shall learn the truth in due time. Choose ye out two more men and watch over them, keep them safe. It may be we employ the same enemy and, if so, we may have discovered a great ally."

"Yes, Sir," answered Artemas.

"I go to camp. I have a feeling some of our scouts may arrive soon with other news." With that, the dark figure signaled the rest of the men to follow, and they stole away through the trees silently.

As Albert, Johanan, and the girls slept, Brin kept a watchful eye, not knowing three other pairs of unseen eyes were likewise keeping watch over him.

A Hidden People

Sir Marcus and his men arrived back at their village just as the last embers of daylight faded into the darkness of night. "Gilbert, have any scouts returned to report?"

"No, Sir, none as of yet."

"Keep a close watch; I suspect other news will arrive soon."

"Yes, Sir."

Sir Marcus turned aside into his hut to think. *If my guess is near the mark, they won't be too far behind. We will need a couple of days to prepare, three would be better, but two will be sufficient. Maybe we could buy us some time. Yes. But in the end, we shall need help.* Just outside the hut door, Gilbert called, interrupting his thoughts.

"Sir Marcus!"

"Enter."

"Sir, you were correct. Our scout from the south has just arrived. He spotted a company at least 500 strong just outside the southern border."

"How far away?" Sir Marcus asked.

"Two days, maybe three. There seems to be some reluctance within their camp." Gilbert continued with a confidant grin. "It appears they halted because of disagreements as to whether or not they should enter our little forest."

A smile crossed Sir Marcus's face as he said, "Splendid. That is all the time we shall need, especially with the element of fear on our side. It would help to reduce their numbers a bit. An army of five hundred troops hardly seems a healthy balance against our two hundred and three. I would certainly like to balance the scales before we engage in the conflict."

"Sir," Gilbert interjected, "numbers certainly do not win a battle. But we are only two hundred men. You must be speaking of our three other visitors, yes? And why would three more make any difference?"

"Yes, I speak of our visitors, and they will indeed make a difference, a huge difference. Trust Me!"

Camp for Sir Marcus was a small village of crudely built huts nestled secretly behind a clever wall of thicket made up of rhododendron and other plants so thickly interwoven that even the light of campfires on the other side couldn't penetrate the dense foliage. There were only two entrances into camp – one under, like a sort of tunnel, and one over the thicket by a network of vines and tree branches. Both were heavily guarded and well camouflaged. One would never see the entrance in the thicket unless he fell into it, and the other way over the thicket was nearly invisible. Sir Marcus lived in this mysterious secret village with two hundred of his countrymen and some of their families. Exciting as it may seem, this was no easy existence. Sir Marcus and his people had fled to the wood to find safety during their exile from the kingdom of Avery.

When they first arrived in Wylderland, an old man came out to meet them, a hermit named Nicolas, who befriended them and took them into his fellowship. Nicolas taught them much about survival in the dark and foreboding forest; what could be eaten; what was poisonous; and what plants could be used for medicine. He taught them how to make use of everything around them. He taught them to recognize the best hemp for fibers to twist into bow strings; how to fashion arrows from cedar wood; and even where to find the best flint for making arrowheads.

The exiles of Avery were for the most part military men with a few farmers mixed in as well. Nicolas stayed with the company until they were well established and very capable of survival in the dense forest. Then one day he simply said goodbye, walked away, and never looked back. Most had already figured that village life was much too formal and close knit for a loner such as Nicolas, and they were all very thankful for the time and help he had so graciously given them. Those who knew him best knew better than waste their time trying to figure him out but held their peace and hoped they would meet again in time.

The exiles adapted very well to life in the forest and even began to flourish there. They perfected the skill of tree climbing and learned how to move gracefully from tree to tree. As silent as a ghost, the young men could glide from limb to limb, blending ever so skillfully into the branches around them. The tree men, as they were often called, were responsible for harvesting most of the wild game that fed the entire village, but their craft and skill soon proved essential for their very existence.

Their forest was an old one – as old as time itself. Ax had never been laid against any tree of Wylderland. They were left to grow tall and strong with huge branches spread outward and sturdy limbs that would meet one another and were thick enough in some places for two men to stand side-by-side and cross from one tree to another. Vines were in plenty, so other limbs could be connected by woven ladders. The men gathered the smaller vines and braded them tightly to make strong rope, so when the branches failed to provide passage, they simply tied these ladders wherever they were needed. In this manner, they built an ingenuous overhead travel system high above the forest floor where they could traverse almost all of their borders. From the forest floor, this extensive passageway system looked completely natural. Unless shown, one would never even know it existed.

With the help and wisdom of Nicolas and the leadership of Sir Marcus, they were able to survive. At night around the campfire, the old hermit, Nicolas, had entertained the villagers with stories about a great bear who long ago reigned as king of this very forest.

It was these fantastic tales of the "King of the Wood" that inspired Sir Marcus with an ingenious idea. He would create for himself a new identity. For the protection of the woodsmen it would be most helpful to detour any travelers or unwanted visitors away from Wylderland altogether. What better way than by filling the hearts and minds of superstitious old busybodies with plenty of talk about bears and bones. So, over time, with some skeletal remains of a feral ox and a few well-placed scratch marks, Sir Marcus would become "The Bear King."

Fear in the Night

Brin finished the first watch of the night, and even tarried at his post much longer than usual and took half of the next watch as well. His mind was aboil with thoughts. Sleep would not come, so it was just as well to let the others rest. He was amazed at how well the children had taken the news and how neither girl had even mentioned the fact that they were princesses. That thought seemed to have escaped them totally – never entered into their minds. The only thing that seemed to matter to them was the fact that they were sisters. It puzzled him at first, and then he began to understand.

Even though they were very young when separated, each had always had a void in her heart that only the other could fill. It was as if each had known a piece of herself was missing, though neither had understood it. He pondered how it was the same with God and man – how we were created in His image and then separated by the fall of our father Adam and all carry this void or empty place in our heart that only God can fill, even though most people never understand it. So Brin had simply sat, watched, thought, and prayed, thanking God once again for answered prayer.

Johanan wiped the sleep from his eyes as he took his place at watch. He hardly had his wits about him yet when suddenly a howl, shrill and bone-jarring, sounded in the deep. He jumped up, sword ready, and called to Brin: "Captain!"

"Yes, I heard it, Johanan," Brin said. "He is close and probably not alone." Before Brin had finished his words, another howl came from a different direction.

"You know, I just hate it that you are right all the time! Why couldn't you be wrong, just this once?"

"It's a benefit of advanced age," Brin answered, his tone light.

Albert appeared from the darkness. "We have company, I hear."

"Sounds like it," Johanan said.

"Did it wake the children?" Brin asked.

"No," Albert said. "They are exhausted. Let's hope they won't wake."

Another howl came from yet another direction.

Johanan said, "It seems our furry friends are interested in a meal, and we are the main course." He turned and looked at Brin. "They probably don't know you are old meat and tough."

"You've not had aged beef, I take it," Brin said. Then he turned to Albert. "You had better go stoke the fire with what wood is left; then keep watch from that direction. Johanan, you watch this way, and I shall check on the horses and watch from there. It looks as if we have all had such sleep as we will tonight."

The horses were spooked and pulled on their lead ropes and stamped their hooves. Brin did his best to calm them, but was hard put to it. Nothing can strike fear in the heart of man or beast like the roar of a lion or the howl of a wolf. With each call, the beasts seemed to be getting closer, and the horses tried that much harder to break away and run. Brin was at the end of his rope and didn't know how much longer the lines would hold. Then came a final yowl that sounded less than a stone's throw away and ... that was it. The horses snapped the ropes, broke free, and ran for their lives. Brin was blessed not to get trampled in the fray.

With all the noise the children woke. Albert yelled for them to stay close to the fire. Terrified, they sat clinging to each other. Eve kept her head buried in Dawn's hair, too frightened to look and doing her best not to scream. Dawn was scared, too, and held on tight to Eve but kept a watchful eye despite her fear.

Johanan's heart was pounding as he prepared himself for the attack, thinking: *First a bear king, now wolves! I warned him, but would he listen to me? No! Well, makes no matter now, does it? But... You know, now that I think of it, a couple of wolf hides would be a good thing to take back and show the men. Yes! That would make up for any tales of my screaming if someone happened to tell on me.* With new enthusiasm Johanan began to call, "Here, boy. Here, little wolfie. Come now, my little fellow."

Albert's mind was fixed on one thought – protecting his little girl. There was no question now – he would gladly give his own life to save hers. Her safety was the only thing that mattered. When another howl came he thought to himself: *They are almost here, it won't be long now.*

The attack never came. The men stood around the camp back-to-back, swords drawn, until the break of day. The children had eventually fallen asleep again in each others' arms.

"Well, it seems our visitors have had a change of heart," Albert said, breaking the silence.

"Seems that way," Brin agreed. "But, I wonder why."

"Maybe they decided to have horse for dinner instead," Albert added.

"Let's hope not," Johanan said downcast. "I have no desire to walk the rest of the way through these accursed woods."

"We have no choice now," Brin said. "So we may as well get started." He added, "Here, have a saddle!"

"Great!" was all Johanan could say.

It was slow going that morning with each man carrying a saddle over one shoulder and a pack over the other. The children did their best to help carry what they could.

Eve was heartbroken and worried sick about Magi. She loved that horse. He had been a very real and important part of her life ever since she could remember. He was more than her father's war horse; he was part of the family, and all her thought was bent on him. She tried not to let her fears show. She did her best to be brave and face the tasks at hand. Noticing Dawn struggling with the load she was trying to carry, Eve rushed over to help. She was a strong sturdy girl, and knowing that her younger sibling was still rather weak, Eve carefully took most of the load from Dawn without even letting her know it.

Brin watched from a distance and marveled at what he saw. He was very well aware that Eve was heartsick over losing Magi, yet still did all she could to care for her sister. He couldn't have been more proud of his little girl. *Yes*, he thought, *she will always be my little girl*. Then he knelt down and took Eve by the hand and so tenderly said, "Don't you worry about Magi. He has been in far bigger scrapes than this. He knows how to take care of himself, and you know what else?"

"What, Father?"

"He will also take care of the other horses; he knows how to lead them to safety. So stop your fretting, all right?"

"You really think he is safe?"

"I am sure of it."

They hadn't traveled far from camp when Albert spotted blood on the ground. Seeing it, Eve started to cry, terrified it might be from Magi, just then they found a large clump of grey fur.

"This hair looks to be wolf" Albert announced.

"What did I tell you?" Brin said to Eve. "Looks like the wolves came to a bad end, not the horses." Then they spotted more blood, then more fur. They were all perplexed. What could have happened? Why didn't those wolves attack them in the night? It just didn't make sense. They had more questions than answers, but one thing was certain – they were all very thankful not to have been eaten by wolves the night before. Amazed and puzzled, they all wondered in their minds, as they slowly wandered down the old path through the forest, not knowing what new danger lay ahead.

Friendly Guides

"Captain."

"Yes, Johanan."

"Have you noticed anything strange today?"

"What? Something strange in this forest, whatever could you mean?"

"I am in earnest. It seems as if ... well, I don't know. Oh, never mind."

"He speaks of the movement overhead," Albert interrupted, cutting his eyes upward.

"So you noticed?" Brin answered. He then turned to Dawn and asked, "And what say ye, our young scout?"

Dawn calmly answered, "We are not alone, but I know not yet what it is."

Johanan continued, "I couldn't be sure what the movement was. I thought maybe there was some strange bird about, but I haven't seen or heard any unusual birds."

"We have had company all morning," Brin said, his voice calm and calculated. They seem to be before and behind,"

"Could it be Lucian has overtaken us already?" Johanan asked.

Brin shrugged. "Well, it certainly could be, but I don't believe it is. First of all, the sorts of men who ride with Lucian are not exactly what one might call *skillful*. Granted, he does have a few good soldiers on his side, but the greater part of his men are better suited to stealing some poor farmer's pig than moving stealthily through the forest. Whoever or whatever we have encountered here today possesses a greater skill than I have learned," Brin added with admiration in his voice.

Albert joined in and said, "Gentlemen, I am inclined to believe we shall soon meet the famous Bear King of Wylderland."

At that, Johanan dropped his pack and drew his sword.

Brin laughed and said, "Sheath your sword, my friend. If battle was what it sought, it would have been joined before now."

"I agree." Albert continued, "Whatever it is just seems to be watching and following us. It has made no attempt to stop our passage or even slow us down. It feels more like a guide than an enemy."

"Which is exactly why we shall continue onward," Brin said. "But to be safe, Ladies, stay close at hand."

Eve answered, "You don't have to warn us twice, Father!"

They walked on slowly till nearly midday, each in great anticipation as to what would happen next. Outwardly Brin and Albert were both solid as a rock, aware of things happening around them yet calm and in total control. Johanan kept turning this way and that, sweating, heart pounding, more uncertain than he had ever been. Johanan was no doubt a capable and valiant young man and what he lacked in experience, he more than made up for in raw courage, but something about all this was tormenting to him. He could meet nearly any foe, face to face, but the unknown and the unseen nature of this encounter, was driving him, with each passing moment, to the edge of madness. Yet amidst the inner turmoil the calmness and assurance of his superiors spoke volumes to his soul. He was accustomed to facing an opponent he could see and predict. Here he knew not who the enemy was, and, even worse, *what* it was. There was so much he didn't know, but he knew he was blessed to be in the presence of two great men.

Eve stayed so close she almost walked on Brin's heals, afraid to look up, terrified what she might see. Dawn walked close behind Albert. Her choice crushed Johanan, yet he understood. He knew she was happy to be close to her father.

She was in fact happier than she had ever been. She was wanted, even loved, and off on a grand adventure. What more could a little girl ask for? She had of course spotted the movement overhead but had chosen not to say anything because she knew how her sister mourned in her heart for Magi. She also saw the fear in her face and didn't want to frighten her anymore than she already was.

Finally, it happened. The figure of a man dropped from a tree directly in front of the company not 30 feet away.

"Hail, Lord Brin and company! I hope you are having a pleasant journey?"

"Indeed we are," Brin answered. He cocked his head and continued. "And to whom do we owe our thanks and gratitude for such a fine escort as we have enjoyed?"

"Aw, so you noticed your silent guardians? We must needs improve our skills if we have been so easily detected."

"If you improved your skills, you would have to become ghosts in the wind," Brin answered.

"A hearty compliment that is, coming from such a great and noble warrior as yourself. My thanks to you." Even though the conversation, as peculiar as it was, had thus far been rather lighthearted and friendly, Brin, Albert, and Johanan kept their hands on the hilt of their swords. Johanan would have already charged had the calmness and gentle tone of his captain's speech not quieted his fevered zeal.

The speaker continued. "Please allow me to properly introduce myself. My name is Artemas. If I may, the Lord of this forest, The Bear King, requests your presence, and it is at this point that ye must abandon this old path. If you would kindly follow me, I assure you no one in your company is in any danger." When he finished speaking, several more men dropped from the trees all around them. They were surrounded.

Brin replied, "Well, seeing as we have traveled with you thus far, I see no reason not to follow you."

Artemas laughed then, said, "Come, you must be hungry. We shall provide you with a hot meal, good conversation, and some vital information."

Johanan finally relaxed and said, "A hot meal, you say? Now that's a kindly gesture if ever I heard one!"

Their new guide Artemas then turned and moved just a few more steps down the old path. The company fell in line behind him followed by the remainder of the mysterious woodsmen. Artemas then left the trail and headed directly into the thickest part of the forest. Brin had to keep on his toes to keep up with their new guide, who seemed to glide through the brush without disturbing a leaf or making the slightest sound. Though Brin had no idea who these woodsmen were, where they came from, or how they acquired such skill, he certainly admired them.

Johanan turned and spoke to Albert, "If they got any better they would have to be ghosts, huh! I'm not so sure they're not ghosts! I've never seen anything like it. We sound like a gaggle of mad geese compared to these fleet-footed men!"

Albert just laughed and responded, "Look and learn, my son, look and learn."

FRIENDSHIP RENEWED

When they arrived at the multi-flowered thicket just outside the hidden village, Artemas stopped and said, "Wait here," then seemingly vanished among the twigs and leaves. A few seconds later he reappeared and said, "Follow me." He and another of the woodsmen then took hold of some branches and moved an entire section of the thicket to reveal the tunnel through the hedge. Once through, the company found themselves in the middle of a populated forest village.

Then Eve screamed with delight, "Magi!" Sure enough, there stood Magi and the other horses tied to a tree with vine rope. They were all amazed.

"Do wonders never cease?" Johanan said, thinking out loud.

"Yes, your horses are just fine. A little weary from their fright but just fine nevertheless. That big boy there led them right here," he said, pointing to Magi. "We found them waiting on the other side of the thicket in the night. I suppose he followed our scent." Brin looked at Eve and just smiled and winked.

The village was truly something to behold. One could never have imagined people living virtually invisible right in the middle of this forest. The encampment was crude yet clean and extremely fortified. Everything was so well-hidden they knew they would never have found this site had they not been led to it. As they looked around in wonder at all the faces looking back at them, a hut door opened and out stepped a man of Brin's own age and a young lad about 12 years old. The older was dressed in clothes that had once been quite fair and spoke of some degree of dignity but now were ragged and tattered by toil and harshness of life in the wood. The leather arm bands, belt, and scabbard he wore were plain and unadorned yet obviously made of skillful craft. The boy was dressed plainer, but the leather he wore was of the same craftsmanship and style. He carried no sword, but a bow and a quiver full of arrows was slung across his back.

"Lord Brin! You and your company are most heartily welcome!"

Brin replied, "Sir Marcus, is that you?"

"Yes, yes, it is I."

"So *you* are the Bear King?"

"Guilty as charged," Sir Marcus responded as he bowed his head. "And this young man is my son Mikael."

"But why? I can't get over the fact it's you. How?" Brin asked.

"I shall explain all in due time, but may I enquire as to who are these who accompany you? Albeit the children here need no introduction; I believe they are the longlost offspring of King Amasa and the good Queen Grace, are they not?"

"Yes, indeed they are. Sir Marcus, I'd like you to meet Eve and her sister Dawn. This is Lord Albert; he commands the band of soldiers that hail from the west of the castle. This is Johanan, the best soldier in my regiment, as well as my right hand. Both are good and honorable men." Brin glanced at the members of his company. "I would like to introduce to you all Sir Marcus, the best and most trusted knight of King Ahyarm, Lord of the kingdom of Avery, which lies to the East of this forest. We fought together during your father's time, Johanan, against the heathen kingdom of the Eglonites from the north, when they descended upon us and thought to devour the whole land for themselves. Our armies joined forces in the war for we were hard against each other...."

"...And together victory was ours," Sir Marcus cut in.

They all exchanged greetings as the children curtsied and then Brin said, "First, I must thank you and your men, for I assume they were our protectors from the wolves during the night, and also for the care of our horses."

"You are most welcome. I understand the wolves gave you quite a restless night, but I assure you that you were in no danger; as a matter of fact, you were all very well looked after. Artemas here is as fine an archer in the night as he is in the day."

"So what is this all about? Your king is an honorable man, so what are you doing living as the Bear King in the middle of this dreadful forest?"

Sir Marcus turned, opened the door of the hut, smiled, and said, "Come in, sit and eat, refresh yourselves, and I shall finish my tale."

They all waited until Eve hugged Magi and kissed him on the nose, and then they entered the hut to find a feast fit for a king spread out upon a rough wooden table. There was roast venison, stewed rabbit, wild berries, bread, and cheese all freshly prepared specially for them.

Johanan elbowed Albert and whispered, "I don't care if they *are* ghosts; this feast looks and smells real enough to me!"

"And we have you to thank, young man," said Sir Marcus.

"Whatever do you mean?" Johanan asked, stunned.

"That scream of yours scared the poor deer you were following so much that he ran right into one of my men!" The whole place erupted with laughter! When they could finally contain themselves, they all took a seat round the table.

Brin asked Sir Marcus, "Of your courtesy, I should like to return thanks before we start. May I?"

"But I just thanked the young man." Sir Marcus laughed a hearty laugh again then added, "I'm not a praying man myself, but please feel free. Mayhap it might do me some good."

Setting the Trap

As the company enjoyed the glorious meal, their host Sir Marcus spoke openly of their plight and cause of the present situation. "So, as you see, it is all very simple. When King Amasa banned Lucian from the realm of Peacehaven, he simply headed east to the kingdom of Avery. In little or no time at all, he wormed his way into the king's court and poisoned the mind of good King Ahyram against many of his most loyal soldiers. He then began to solicit men of the baser sort with bribes and lies, and before we understood the depth of his deception, Lucian had already gained much influence and access to untold resources. As you know, the clever sort can be quite convincing. Those of our company have all been slandered and falsely accused in a most vicious manner, and therefore we have been banished to live in exile."

"Treachery, indeed!" Brin said.

Sir Marcus continued. "Indeed. Yet in spite of the lies and treachery of Lucian, all who remain here and under my command are forever loyal to King Ahyram, though he has yet to realize it. Everyone here understands that our king is truly a good man who has alas simply been deceived. We came to the forest to live in peace with our families until all rights could be restored and we could clear our names, prove our loyalty to our king, and see the usurper Lucian defeated."

"What of all this 'Bear King' business?" Johanan had to ask.

Sir Marcus laughed and said, "We took advantage of the old stories of this place and crafted our own legend to ensure our families' safety, and it has worked quiet splendidly. Most would never venture over our borders, and those who do brave them are quickly scared off. In fact, it has already served your purpose well."

"What do you speak of?" Lord Brin asked, puzzled.

"And now to business," Sir Marcus said, changing his tone as he continued. "As we speak, there is a company of five hundred men just on the inside of our borders, led by Lucian himself."

"So he did follow me," Albert said out loud, yet talking to himself.

"Yes, it would seem so. Lord Brin, if I may be so bold as to suggest, it would seem that once again it would be profitable to your company, as well as mine, for us to join forces as before, for we share a common adversary."

"So what do you propose?" Brin asked.

"My soldiers are already at work to even the odds a bit, shall we say, buying us some precious time. Those left in the village are already hard at work gathering materials, making arrows, and stockpiling stones for the slingers."

"Slingers?" Albert enquired with a doubtful look.

"Yes, I have fifty men who can sling a stone at a hair's breadth, with either right or left hand. Granted, it is a bit crude, but I assure you it is most effective. Once a quiver is empted, it is empty, but when arrows are spent, stones are easy to find and prove to be just as lethal, in the right hands."

"That is quite ingenious," Albert said in awe. "I would love to learn such a skill. Once in a battle, I loosed all my arrows, threw my dagger, and broke my sword. I had to finish the brawl with nothing but fist and sword hilt. If I could learn to sling...." Albert said, drifting off in his own thoughts.

"I will have my best man, Gilbert, show you what he knows, but for now, back to the business at hand. I have a plan. For the moment, we have the element of fear on our side, and as I said, my men are using it to our advantage to delay Lucian even as we speak. As of last evening the army was encamped at our southern border. Counting the time my men may afford us by delaying Lucian's troops, and the half day already gone, I believe we have just enough time left."

"Time left for *what*, exactly?" Brin asked.

"To be arrayed, prepared, and in position for full battle. To the north of us, in the direction you were traveling along the old path, there is an area where the forest thins and there are many rocky outcroppings. I believe that is the most advantageous place for battle. I shall place a contingent of men in the surrounding trees, and the rest behind the rock face. But we will need your company to lead them there."

"And we will be leading them into a trap," Johanan replied, his voice excited.

"Precisely," Sir Marcus said. "I feel the time has come. We must face Lucian head on, once and for all."

"Well," Brin began, "it seems you have thought this through well enough." There followed a few moments of silence as Sir Marcus allowed Lord Brin to think. He stood up, and walked around the hut milking his chin. "You say Lucian has five hundred riding with him, eh? How many men are in your command?"

"We are two hundred, but if you would so allow, Sir, counting your company that makes two hundred and three."

Johanan spoke up again and said, "Eerie woods full of ghosts, bear kings, and wolves I'm not so keen about, but facing the evil that occasioned the death of my father and his army, outnumbered two to one, in strange terrain, being left in the open as bait on a hook, well now that is my kind of fight! What are we waiting for?" Johanan's voice had reached a fevered pitch.

"Well," Sir Marcus said to Brin, "your right hand certainly has plenty of zeal, but are you sure it is not the foolish braggadocio of his youth?"

"Believe me, Sir Marcus, his braggadocio is exceeded only by his courage and ability."

"That's what I was hoping you would say," replied Sir Marcus.

Brin continued. "My greatest concern is for the children. Using them as a decoy puts them at great risk. Above all else, they *must* be kept safe."

"My men will do all in their power to ensure the children's safety, but for the trap to work, they must be part of the bait," Sir Marcus answered. "For they are what Lucian is coming after."

At this point Dawn walked over to Brin and said, "If he has been following us this whole time, we have already been in great danger. Nothing is any different from what it has already been. Only now we know things of a surety, and we are blessed with brave new friends. Don't worry about us; we shall be just fine. You said yourself that coming to Wylderland was the Lord's will, so, the will of the Lord be done." She then went to her sister and laid her arm across her shoulder.

Eve agreed and said, "Yes, Father, don't worry about us. You must do what you must."

"Well," said Brin soberly, "I believe the fair ladies have decided for me. Let's get to work then, shall we?"

EVIL ENSUES

"What is the meaning of this?" Lucian barked to Karl, his captain in command. "Why are these sluggards pitching camp instead of marching forward? I gave no such order. These worthless blighters are costing me precious time!"

"I gave the order. Our horses are spent and so are the men. You've driven them brutally for the past three days and nights, gaining time I might add, and, considering what some of the men are saying, if you would like to keep your little army here, you would be wise to hold your tongue. Besides, do you not know where we are? This is the border of Wylderland."

"I don't care whose land it is, nor do I care what these insolent sots you call soldiers are saying. But what I *do* care about is that the daughters of Amasa along with their feeble custodians have not been found and we are wasting precious time. Do you understand?"

"You are not listening to me. I'm telling you – this is Wylderland! Have you not heard the stories of this place?"

"Stories! I care nothing for children's tales!"

"This is no child's play. People talk of a great force that rules this forest and suffers no intruders."

"Ridiculous blather, all of it!" snorted Lucian.

"Ridiculous or not, there isn't a man here who hasn't heard a strange tale or two of this place. I have known some myself who have disappeared in these woods never to be seen again. And, to be perfectly honest, the men are not taking kindly to the thoughts of entering said forest."

"You listen to me: I will give you exactly until sunup, at which time you will have every man in this army saddled and ready. That little company entered this forest, and we will pursue them until we overtake them." Then leaning into the captain's face with menacing eyes and a threatening tone, he added, "Your future depends on it. Do you understand?"

"Understood," Karl snapped back in reply. Lucian bit his lip, turned, and went away in a rage. Karl threw his pack to the ground and grumbled under his breath.

Because of itching ears, word spread quickly among the men of the plan for the next day. Most were, to say the least, not happy.

There was a great deal of storytelling that night around the campfires. Each man shared his own version of the horrors of Wylderland, and as their fear grew wider, the tales grew taller. Those among them who possessed the hardest of hearts mocked the fearful and others joined in, mainly in an attempt to cover up their own terror. As the fires died down, so did the talk, leaving each man with his own thoughts. In the darkest hour of the night, several men stole away. The watchmen who were on duty turned a blind eye to the deserters, wishing in earnest they themselves had the courage to do the same.

Sunrise came, and with it emerged Lucian from the safe and secure hole in which he had hid for the night. He was his normal cheerful self. "Captain! Captain! Why are these men not ready as I ordered?! Why are they still mulling about? I warned you!"

"Yes, as a matter of fact you did, and I in turn, warned *you!* At least twenty men packed and left during the night, and another fifty are unaccounted for. Their horses and gear remain, but their whereabouts are unknown, and finally there is this—" Karl pointed to the ground and there they were: enormous bear tracks. Huge, bigger than life and even bigger than any of the fireside tales could have told. They came out from the edge of the woods, followed down the outermost edge of the camp, and then led back into the woods. Everywhere the prints led lay the disheveled bed rolls and gear of the missing men.

"What's going on here?" Lucian demanded. "What do the sentinels say? Why did they not sound the alarm?"

"The watchman from this side of camp is one of the missing men. The others neither saw nor heard anything during the night."

"Enough of this rubbish! Get this army moving. Now!"

"Yes, Sir." Karl then turned toward the listening soldiers. "All right, men, finish packing and mount up!" The men hesitated and stood motionless for a brief moment as each read the others' faces in search of some answer to the bizarre events unfolding around them. When the captain noticed their indecision, he yelled, "You heard the order! Now! Mount up! We ride!" The men frantically started throwing the rest of their gear together, and within minutes the first ranks of Lucian's army were entering the border of Wylderland.

As they traversed the narrow forest path, Lucian's patience soon wore thin.

"Captain! Why are we moving so slowly?! Do you not know how to drive a pack of lazy dogs?"

Struggling to constrain his anger, Captain Karl responded, "Sir, open terrain is one thing, but this forest is dense, dark, and strange to these men. They are doing the best they can under the circumstances."

"Then I suggest you send a few men ahead to scout things out. Maybe that would soothe the minds of these timid toddlers you call soldiers and speed things up!"

"As I have said before, if you want to keep these 'timid toddlers' of yours, you had better learn to tame your tongue."

Lucian was fuming on the inside but decided to stay his tongue and allow Karl to pass on ahead of him. Rather than worsen his already frustrated condition by dwelling on the incompetence of others, as he deemed it, he decided to occupy his mind with dreams of the revenge he had planned. He was engulfed in his own evil black thoughts when a commotion startled him. Suddenly about a dozen men went riding past him as fast as they could. As the last man passed by, Lucian recognized him as one of the advance scouts Karl had sent, and he had a look of sheer terror on his face.

"What is the meaning of this?" he shouted. The entire company had stopped. As Lucian made his way to the front of the column, he could hear whisperings and murmurings. They had reached the first scratch marks. "What is the problem?!!"

"You can see for yourself," Karl replied calmly, as he pointed to the marks.

Lucian spoke in a low, slow, menacing tone. "All I see are some scratches on a tree. That is all. We shall continue onward, unless you are as cowardly as the children who just fled. If that be the case, it will be my pleasure to appoint a new captain. But be of good comfort, I shall see to it that any family you leave behind shall be notified officially of your untimely demise."

Karl looked straight into Lucian's black eyes for a moment before turning and calling out, "Forward!"

Lucian chuckled aloud and said, "I thought so."

Karl ignored this remark. He simply selected another scout, whispered something in his ear, and spurred his horse onward at a good speed until he was first in line. After the scouts had passed out of sight, he then slowed down and set the pace for the rest of the men, a very slow pace. His face was hard as if set in stone, for in his heart, at that very moment, something had changed. He thought to himself as he rode, *I shall not forget that threat or the fact that he called me coward.*

Lucian kept his usual place toward the back of the line and continued to encourage himself in his evil manner. The last few years of counterfeit service, first to King Amasa and then to King Ahyarm, had taken quite a toll on him. In the beginning, feigned loyalty came quite natural for such an accomplished liar as Lucian. He counted it as sport to toy with truth, in such a manner as to stroke his arrogant ego, but now he was bored with his games, and life for Lucian had become quite difficult. Pretending to care for things that meant nothing to him, professing to be kind and gentle, while playing the part of a loyal councillor, had drained him beyond measure. Lucian was thirsty for power, and it felt good to finally be in control, to lay aside all constraint and pretense, and alas be free to be his wicked self. A person can only go on pretending for so long before it begins to break one down.

Yes, he thought to himself. *It won't be long now; I shall be free and have my rightful place. I shall rule not only Peacehaven but I will overthrow that doddered excuse of a king, Ahyarm. Then I will unite and rule both kingdoms! My might and power shall have no end!*

Iron Sharpeneth Iron

That first night in the forest village, Lord Brin and his weary companions enjoyed some much needed rest and slept unusually late, until the morning sun was already bright and adorned by a clear blue sky. It was a beautiful day, the kind of day that makes one happy just to be alive, even when you don't know exactly why. It took a few minutes to stir and wipe the sleep from their eyes, but everyone's spirits seemed high, especially Johanan's, as he awoke to the glorious smell of a bountiful breakfast cooking on a bed of hot coals just outside the door of the little hut. One of the village lads brought a wooden pale of water for washing hands and face, and the girls soon found themselves feeling quite at home. After washing up and having their morning meal, Brin soon broke the idle chatter and informed them all that the time had come for them to go to work.

"Good morning, Mikael," Eve said as she walked out of the hut door into the courtyard.

"Good morning, Your Highness," Mikael replied with a slight bow.

"Why do you call me that?" Eve asked, puzzled.

"You are a princess, are you not?" came his reply.

"I suppose so, but this is all very new to me; besides, I haven't come into the kingdom as of yet, so please call me Eve."

"As you wish, Your High-, I mean, Eve."

"Are you preparing to go somewhere?"

"Yes, my friends and I have our jobs to do. We must go into the woods and gather supplies for making arrows. We know where a group of wild turkeys roost and are going there to look for feathers." Wanting to sound impressive, he added, "Although some say goose feathers make the best arrows, they are harder to find, and we have learned to make do with what we have."

"If my father agrees, may my sister and I come with you?"

"Well…," he hesitated, before adding, "mind you don't get in the way; this isn't play, you know, but serious man's work."

"Yes, of course, we understand. We shall be no trouble at all," Eve said, glancing at Dawn and winking ever so slightly. The girls then ran to ask permission. Sir Marcus saw the concern on Brin's face and put him at ease, assuring him they would be quite safe. So off they went, Eve and Dawn following the group of older children out of the confines of the village and into the forest.

As they walked, Eve spoke, "Mikael?"

"Yes, Eve?"

"I've been wondering about that bow you carry. I've never seen anything like it. It's not at all like the one my father has or the one Johanan carries. It is much shorter and the ends curl outward instead of inward. Where in the world did you get it?"

"I made it! Or rather my father helped me make it. All we woodsmen carry such bows. Nicolas the hermit taught our people how to make them when our old ones began to break and dwindle in number. He is very wise and knows many things. This shorter bow is much easier to handle while running through the woods and is just as powerful as the old long bows. When everything is put to right, I shall one day be a knight of Avery and command the entire division of archers in our army, and everyone under my command shall carry a bow like mine!"

Eve became silent for a while before saying, "I hope all is put to right soon so you and all the woodsmen can return home."

Young Mikael replied sadly, "Me, too, Eve. Me, too." Then suddenly his face lightened up a bit and he said, "But living in this forest hasn't been all bad. Had we stayed at home, I would have seen very little of father."

"I know what that feels like," Eve told him.

Mikael continued as though he hadn't heard her. "But here I have been his right hand, and he says he couldn't do without me. For us woodsmen to survive in the forest everyone must do what he can. Even the small children have tasks suitable for them. We must all work together and do our part."

"You are all truly amazing," Eve said with great admiration.

Mikael just smiled and walked a bit straighter, held his head a little higher, and stuck his chest out just the slightest degree further, being very glad the "women folk" had come along after all. It wasn't long before Mikael was holding Eve's hand, leading her through his domain, with Dawn in tow, giggling to herself and trying hard not to be noticed.

In this way, the girls spent the day helping the older children as they searched for the raw materials they needed, ever mindful of the seriousness of their task, but far from understanding the tragedy of war and the fierceness of battle that would soon be upon them.

Late in the afternoon when they returned, the girls tried their hand at making arrows. Nicolas had taught the villagers how, of course, and the women had become masters of the art. They welcomed their young helpers and rather enjoyed their company. The girls proved to be very helpful, but it was much more than that. They brought with them hope – hope that somehow, by the grace of God, the village could be delivered from a life of exile and begin a bittersweet journey home.

For the moment, these noble thoughts never occurred to Dawn, who became quite good at stripping the feathers from the quill. Her small fingers were perfect for such tedious work. She also had a good eye for finding any imperfections in the shafts.

Eve worked with a candle to heat the curved shafts for straightening, and also found she could set the point almost as true as the older women. With everyone working together, soon there was a goodly supply of arrows fletched and made ready for the archers.

Johanan spent the day with Artemas and several of the bowmen and delighted in the opportunity to teach them some very impressive hand-to-hand combat techniques he had developed on his own. This proved to be very helpful for the confidence of the woodsmen, for until now, valiant as they were, the woodsmen had never truly met a military resistance and relied heavily on hiding in the trees and generally avoiding most armed confrontations. The woodsmen, in turn, taught him what they could about how to move through the forest unseen and unheard. Johanan was brave as a lion and well-seasoned in full frontal warfare, but like a child he was utterly fascinated by the idea of moving overhead, ghostly and undetected.

Later that evening Johanan told Brin, "Oh how I wish I had more time with these men. I could spend days training them and being trained by them. I have more to learn than I ever knew."

Brin smiled a fatherly smile and replied, "Johanan, you are no doubt learning more than a few clever tricks. Wisdom is better than rubies, and your father would be very proud."

Albert spent most of the day with Gilbert. He found it easy to talk with him, and before he knew what happened, he had opened up and shared all his heart. He told him of his pain, loss, bitterness of soul, and how the Lord had come to him and changed him on the inside. Gilbert understood. He also had shared a similar path in his life compounded by the loss of his standing in life, his good name and honor, and alas his homeland. Albert saw firsthand that no matter your difficulties in this life, there is always someone who has suffered much more. Gilbert enjoyed teaching him the use of the sling, and Albert proved a natural. In no time at all, Albert could hit almost any target Gilbert set before him. What a glorious day they had together slinging stones a while, laughing a while, and crying a while. It had been so long since Albert made a friend he had forgotten what it felt like. By the end of the day, he decided it felt good, very good.

The next day Gilbert presented Albert with a new sling with the image of a bear hand-tooled on the flat. "Here is something to remind you of your time here in the forest. Use it well, and teach others how to use it."

"I will certainly do so," Albert said, as he turned the sling over and over examining it closely. "Thank you. It is beautiful! When did you have time to make it?" Albert asked, amazed.

"Oh, I made it during the night; I couldn't sleep anyway and, besides, you needed one of your own. You have the knack for slinging. I hope it proves useful for you."

Albert grabbed Gilbert's forearm with his and smiled saying, "Thank you again, friend."

Gilbert grasped Albert's arm firmly and said "You are most welcome, my friend."

Brin spent most of the day in council with Sir Marcus, making plans and carefully weighing out every advantage and disadvantage. There was so much to consider, so much to gain and so much to lose. Brin was spiritually mature enough to understand perfectly that what they needed was more than military strategy and human reasoning; they needed supernatural guidance. With this in mind, he slipped away to spend the remainder of the day in secret prayer between the thicket wall and the back of the hut.

As they sat alone later that evening, Brin asked Eve tenderly one last time, "Are you sure you still want to go through with this?"

"Yes, Father," Eve replied. "Don't worry about us. We will be fine. And besides," she continued, "Lucian must be stopped for the good of everyone. It isn't just about me and my sister anymore; these poor people need to be able to return to their homes. If you don't stop Lucian now while all is prepared and ready, who knows the damage he will do when no one is expecting it."

"My darling," Brin said with love and amazement, "where in the world did one so young acquire such wisdom?"

"I was brought up well," she told him. "My father taught me many things." With that, Eve threw herself into his arms.

A tear trickled down Brin's face as he held her close and said, "In my heart, you shall always be my little girl, and I couldn't be more proud of you. I love you."

"And I love you, Father."

BACK ON THE OLD PATH

Early the next morning Albert walked into the hut followed by Dawn and Johanan and announced, "All is ready, the time has come to depart." Brin and company stepped outside to find Magi and the other horses saddled and ready.

Along with the horses stood Sir Marcus smiling as he saluted the brave little band.

"Lord Brin, it seems it is time for our adventure to begin. You know the plan. Gilbert and a couple of the men will lead you to the place where you left the path to come to our village. They shall erase any tracks and see to it there is no trace back toward the village. Once back there you and your company shall continue to travel the old path until you reach the rocky outcroppings. Some of my most trusted men left in the night to make preparations. I will lead the remainder of my men using the overhead passage and be in place before nightfall. From our last reports, my men have done a marvelous job of delaying and reducing Lucian's army. It seems he has lost a good number of soldiers, more than a hundred or so." At that, he laughed a hearty laugh.

"That should certainly help," Brin said.

"Indeed," Sir Marcus agreed. Then he continued. "You should reach the battlefield in the early morning hours, and if the enemy continues at the present pace and does not camp for the night, they should reach the same spot some few hours later or sometime shortly after sunrise. Lucian and his army may indeed camp for the night, but my instinct tells me he will not spare the time. For I hear his patience is growing thin, and he knows he is coming to the end of this forest. I think he would prefer to work his evil in the dark shadows of the woodland rather than in the open plains outside the forest border. If in fact they do camp for the night, you must simply be patient and wait. In either event, you shall have ample time to secure the children and prepare the site as if you had stopped for the night. The success of our entire plan depends upon the enemy's believing he is pursuing a very small number, who have no defense or knowledge of their approach."

Brin said, "It is a good plan, Sir Marcus, and I am truly grateful for all you have done and all the hard work of your people, though I do beg your pardon, but the success of the plan is based upon the will of God." At this statement, Sir Marcus paused briefly to consider the gentle reproof, and held his tongue, and then Brin added, "But be of good cheer, dear friends, the battle is not ours, but the Lord's. And if HE fights for us, who can be against us?"

"I would give a king's ransom to have such remarkable faith as you," Sir Marcus said, his tone sincere and sober.

"But you can have it at far less expense, Sir. In fact it is free. You see, true faith is not a silver trinket that a man may buy and sell or even earn that he might carry it about in his pocket. Faith is a gift from God, free to all who are willing to repent and trust the merits of Christ and Christ alone. Genuine faith is by no means elusive to them who take God at His word. Faith is abundant and available to all who desire it and seek His face with all their heart."

Sir Marcus gazed longingly into the faces of the little company surrounding him, one face at a time, and thought to himself, *These do indeed have something that I do not possess, and inside I have a strange longing to acquire it.* As Gilbert and his men led the company out of the village, the thought occurred to him, *Peace! What I saw in their faces looked a lot like peace.* Suddenly, before he knew what he was doing or why, Sir Marcus ran frantically to catch them before they were out of sight. "Lord Brin, Wait!" The company halted. "I was wondering, when this is all over, maybe we could spend some time together and you could tell me more of this God of yours, and, who knows, maybe I will become a praying man myself."

"With a good will, Sir Marcus, it would be an honor. I shall tell you as much as you wish to hear of my dear Savior. Yet for now, listen closely and perhaps you may hear His voice. If by grace He calls upon your heart, answer swiftly, as best you can. He cares for you, my friend. Trust Him." And with a hearty respect, as a parting gesture, Lord Brin saluted smartly and said, "Farewell."

As Lord Brin and his little troop made their way down the path, Gilbert and his men worked backward and brushed out their tracks. Then, quick as a flash, they shimmied up a tree and onto the overhead passageway.

"Of a certainty," Johanan said, "these men are incredible!"

"Indeed they are," Albert responded still looking overhead. He added, "Let's see if you have learned anything from the woodsmen. How about a contest, you and I? I propose that from here to the outcroppings whoever makes the most noise loses. Agreed?"

"Agreed," Johanan said. "But what shall the prize be to the winner?"

"How about, after the battle, the loser carries all the gear of the winner the remainder of the journey to the castle?"

"So be it, although," Johanan hesitated, "are you sure you want to risk it? That is going to be quite a heavy load for a man of your age."

"There he goes again with the age thing!" Brin, said, laughing.

"We shall see," Albert snickered. "We shall see."

The company traveled on. Brin took the lead, Albert in the middle with the girls, and Johanan brought up the rear. They made sure they were leaving behind a good trail. The children held hands as they walked but did not talk as each was lost in her own thoughts. Albert made not a sound as he walked. He seemed to glide as the woodsmen had done. Johanan was doing his best to be silent but was hard put to it. He thought to himself, *How did Lord Albert pick up on so much so fast? Me and my big mouth. I hope his gear isn't all that heavy.*

Albert was laughing to himself on the inside, having a marvelous time, thinking, *He may be young, but this old dog knows how to learn a new trick. I can't wait to try the new sling Gilbert made me.*

A Rude Awakening

Mortal words could not begin to describe the breathtaking beauty of the palace throne room. The sunrays bathed the scores of golden candlesticks as the flames atop the slender white candles flickered and danced. There were now no paintings of King Amasa and his forbears to deck the walls, but in their places hung beautiful tapestries of red and green with interwoven threads of gold. The throne atop the dais was adorned with sheets of rich red and gold and draped with garlands of green all around. The hall was full to overflowing with couturiers dressed in lavish attire and soldiers arrayed in full battle armor. The golden crown, radiating as the sun itself, with its inlaid diamonds, rubies, and emeralds sat on a pillow of deepest royal blue with golden tassels attached to each corner and set atop a milk-white column positioned to the right side of the throne.

Lucian slowly ascended the steps of the dais, his kingly red robe trimmed in the same deep royal blue flowing out in every direction around him. *At last! At last!* he thought to himself. *The kingdom is all mine.* He stopped at the foot of the throne, turned to face the court, gathered his robe about him and then turned and slowly picked up the crown from its pillow. *I see no need in troubling some pious prophet with my coronation; by my own power I have taken this crown, and I am very well able to put it there myself,* Lucian thought as he began lowering the crown toward his head.

At that very moment, his horse suddenly lunged forward and ran violently into the horse in front of him, abruptly interrupting Lucian's fiendish daydream. The stallion then wielded sideways crushing Lucian's knee into a nearby tree. Finally, in the midst of the commotion, his mount reared out of control, throwing him from the saddle. Lucian tumbled to the ground like a sack of potatoes, smashing his left shoulder into the ground as his horse disappeared into the denseness of the shadowy forest, never to be seen again.

Lucian howled with pain and anger. "What is the meaning of this outburst?!" Behind him a soldier was desperately trying to rein in his horse when Lucian pointed to him and yelled, "You! Soldier! Report!"

The soldier replied, "We were attacked, Sir. Something came raining down on us."

"It appears to be acorns," another soldier responded, a bit timid and unaware how ridiculous his answer sounded. "They came down hard and stung the horses." Three men were thrown from their mounts, not counting Lucian, and at least five more disappeared when their horses ran wild with fright."

Lucian shouted, "What are you, soldiers or children, that you run and hide from a few acorns falling from the trees?" He held his shoulder with one hand and rubbed his knee with the other. Then he pointed to one of the men closest to him and said, "Dismount!" The soldier obeyed and got down from his horse. "Help me up!" Lucian barked, motioning for the man to help him get on the horse he had just dismounted.

"But, Sir, this is my horse," the man began to protest, but this was simply met with more vehement screaming from Lucian as Captain Karl quietly talked with another of the fallen soldiers.

As Lucian's anger began to abate, Karl approached gingerly and said, "Those acorns were not simply falling from the trees. The horses were pelted." He then turned to the dismounted soldier and offered his arm to pull him up to the back of his own horse.

When Lucian saw what was about to take place, he ordered, "The fallen soldiers are to be left behind. No horse carrying two men is going to slow me down."

In utter disgust of the merciless order, Karl simply withdrew his arm and spurred his horse forward as the addled soldiers on the ground frantically called after him.

"You can't just leave us here," they protested. "It will mean certain death!"

The army simply passed on without a word until the bewildered voices could no longer be heard.

Time dragged on as the army followed the old path traveling at little more than a snail's pace. The men were on edge, nervous, or just plain scared. With every step their fear grew, and the more their fear grew, the less they carried themselves like soldiers. More and more they revealed themselves to be the undisciplined pirates they truly were. They began to grumble among themselves, and a few times, some of them nearly came to blows over the most trivial matters – such as getting out of line, getting ahead in line, and following too closely. Such matters suddenly became cause for a fight to the death.

Once again, panic broke out in the midst of the host. Near the center of the column, more horses broke line and went running wild, dodging trees in all different directions. Men were also running as wild as the horses, throwing down their armor, slinging their arms, and flopping around like mad men. Some even ran headlong into trees and through brier thickets. It was quite a chaotic scene – horses neighing, running, bucking and kicking; men screaming, crying, and armor flying.

Captain Karl watched helpless and horrified as utter chaos erupted throughout the ranks. With years of training and living through virtually every experience known to man, nothing could have shocked Karl, but, in all his years, nothing had ever left him quite so speechless and out of countenance. "What in the world?" he muttered under his breath as he surveyed the mayhem. Three hours were lost as Captain Karl tried to restore order and recover as many horses and men as could be found. In a narrow passage near where the commotion had begun, a small group of men stood and carefully inspected an enormous hornet's nest that had fallen through the trees and lay empty and torn on the ground. Another dozen soldiers were gone, and several more were mount-less, swollen and in pain from multiple hornet stings, horse kicks, briar cuts, and tree bruises.

After another hour of traveling down the path, mass hysteria broke out yet again. First, there came loud voices, and then two soldiers with pale white faces came rushing past and then a huge commotion erupted when 40 men in a mad dash forced others aside in a desperate retreat back the way they had come. In the bedlam of confusion and retreating men, Lucian's horse was driven through the low lying branches of a hemlock tree.

"What is it now?!" Lucian thundered.

The advance scouts had just come upon the hanging bones and returned yelling, "Death! Death! There is death up ahead!" That was all that was needed to turn 40 men around. Lucian made his way to the front of the procession once more as the remaining men murmured amongst themselves.

"Now what is it?" Lucian asked as he approached.

Captain Karl motioned for Lucian to follow him. Without uttering a word, Karl, simply pointed through the trees up ahead to the disturbing sight of the hanging bones and the sign of warning. Lucian's heart dropped into his stomach at the gruesome scene, and he became even more hateful and cross, in a feeble attempt to hide his own growing fear. "Did that little company pass this way or not?"

"Yes, they did. We found the remains of a campsite a few rods in that direction," Karl answered as he pointed towards the place of the big tree with its great knurled roots.

"So nothing has changed; we are still just pursuing a very small company through some woods. If another soldier tries to leave this army of mine, I will personally see to it that he receives exactly what he deserves, an arrow to the back. Let him fear *that!*"

"Threaten as you will," Karl said, flatly, "but there is something strange and powerful in these woods, and these men know it. You are fortunate to have this many soldiers remaining. There are yet some things which cannot be bought with silver or gold."

Finally, the sun began to set. Soon darkness descended and the men could no longer see the next step. The army camped as best they could. The men stayed close together. No one wanted to sleep on the outside edge; if sleep would come at all. Most of the men lay awake and listened to the night sounds of the forest. At the first sign of light the next morning, Karl sent out another reluctant scouting party, but this time waited for their return before ordering the rest of the men to mount up. Lucian, of course, grumbled and complained about the lost time, but Karl made no notice. He simply replied that he wanted no more surprises as the previous day.

The scouts returned two hours later and reported they saw nothing but the old path and a very good trail left by the company following it. This made Karl very uneasy. *Something doesn't feel right,* he thought to himself. *Even though we have been gaining on them, we have been far enough behind they should have no idea we are following, so why do I feel like we are walking into a trap? What am I saying? I'm already in a trap, and I see no way out of it. I don't want to be on his side, and if he comes into power, I still don't want to be on his side. Yet I've seen what happens to those who cross him or even seem to be an obstacle in his way. I'm doomed if I stay, and I'm doomed if I leave. How did I get myself into this mess? I don't care how much money he has offered, there is not enough gold in the whole world worth putting up with this odious pig. He calls me coward, yet he sleeps in a trench while my men and I sleep in the open. He rides safely toward the back of the procession while I ride up front....* On and on Captain Karl's thoughts rambled as he rode. Amidst his complaining, he was desperately searching for a way out. Yet, for the moment, he saw none.

The army traveled on slowly without talking for the rest for the day. As the sun's rays started to wane, the men looked forward to a hot meal and the comfort of a campfire. Karl was about to give the order to make camp for the night when he heard Lucian storming up from behind calling his name. *Great,* he thought, *what now?*

"Captain! Has the company left their course?"

"No, Sir, their trail has been quite clearly following the old path."

"Do we not have a full moon tonight?"

"Why, yes, we do...."

"And are the trees not sparser than they were, allowing the light to shine through?"

"Well, yes, I suppose they are...."

"Then what's to keep us from continuing our pursuit?"

Karl made no response; he just gazed stone-faced back at Lucian and then kicked his horse forward.

Getting Ready

Meanwhile Brin's small company reached the rocky outcroppings right on schedule and well ahead of Lucian and his army. Even though there was no outward sign of Sir Marcus and the woodsmen, Brin and Albert could feel their presence. They quickly went to work building a small fire and making a campsite. Johanan dug a small trench behind one of the biggest boulders closest to the protection of the overhead woodsmen. Brin somberly walked the girls to the ditch and instructed them to stay down behind the rock at all costs.

"Stay down and out of sight, no matter what happens," Brin sternly warned the girls. "If the battle should go ill for us, stay hidden until some of the woodsmen come to finish the journey and lead you safely home." After they agreed, Brin prayed a prayer of protection and humbly ask that God's will be done. They all said, "Amen," then shared tearful hugs all round. The children took their place in the trench, and the men piled branches all around to hide them as well as could be. With the girls as safe as possible, the men gathered round the campfire.

"Well, Gentlemen, are we ready?" Brin asked.

"Ready," came the reply. They waited quietly, warming themselves by the fire until the first rays of the morning sun began to penetrate the darkness.

"If Sir Marcus is correct," Johanan said, "they should be arriving anytime now."

"Haven't you heard them?" Albert said. "They arrived five minutes ago. I'm surprised you didn't notice; they made more noise than a band of traveling minstrels,"

The three men continued to stand still as if they were unaware of anything happening around them.

"Very good," Albert said, "we now have a left flank and a right flank in perfect position. And now it's time for the snake to raise his ugly head."

Johanan looked at Lord Albert and frowned. "Aw, you took all the surprise out of it!"

DREADFUL DEEDS

"Lord Lucian," Captain Karl whispered, "the company is just up ahead camped amid a rocky outcropping."

"Do you see two children among them?" Lucian asked, his tone now gleeful.

"The scout says there are three men around a campfire and two small bundles wrapped in blankets. Apparently the children are sleeping."

"Splendid," Lucian sneered. "Splendid, indeed! I have waited a long time for this moment, and now it is finally at hand." Then he made a noise that Karl took for a laugh, but it was a hideous, wicked chortle that made even the great Captain Karl's skin crawl.

"How do you wish to proceed?" Karl asked, trying to shake off the sinking feeling in his stomach.

"Have the men fan out as best they can without being detected. They don't have to get very close; I don't expect there to be any real resistance. What could three men possibly do when confronted by my army—great in number if not in courage? They shall simply do as I command and hand over the children. And when they do: Kill them."

"Simple as that?" Karl asked in a mocking tone.

"Yes, simple as that," Lucian hissed with a subtle slur, then slowly turned aside to savor the moment and bask in his victory.

"Well, well, well, what a merry gathering we have here," Lucian said as he stepped just into view amongst the thickest stand of trees.

"We have only been waiting for you to join the party," Lord Brin answered. With that, Karl knew in his heart that all was not as it seemed.

Oblivious to the error of his premature assumptions, Lucian arrogantly continued. "Waiting for me? Surely you jest, yet I am glad we have, by pure chance, happened upon one another. There is a small matter in which I require your assistance. You have something I greatly desire."

"What could we possibly have that would be of interest to you?" Brin enquired, playing along with the charade.

"Now, now, let's not be coy. The time for play is over. I want the children. Kindly hand them over to me."

"And what makes you think we will just hand them over to you?" Johanan asked.

Lucian made a motion, and Captain Karl stepped into view along with several of his soldiers.

"My little army here makes me think so. You are vastly outnumbered. I suggest you do as I say and no harm shall come to anyone." At this lie, a disturbed look crossed Captain Karl's face as he cut his eyes toward Lucian.

"We hand over the children to you and then just walk away, is that it?" Albert asked.

"Yes, just hand them over to me, and you three can be on your merry way unencumbered."

Brin said, "From the look on your captain's face, I would suspect he has been given different orders, not nearly so hospitable as to allow my men and me to simply walk away unharmed. Orders something to the effect of once you have the children then we are to be slain. Do I not guess close to the mark? It seems your captain may be a more honorable man than you understand, for deceit doesn't seem to sit well with him."

Lucian then turned to Karl, sneering, and with a look that meant no good, replied to Brin, "One needn't worry. There is no impeachment to my captain's honor, for he has none." Karl was wroth and seethed inside, yet at the same time he was overwhelmed with shame and guilt. He hated Lucian, and he hated himself. At that moment something inside him changed and he determined in his heart he would not carry out such orders. If he could find a way to redeem himself, he would do it or die in the attempt. Yes, death would be better than life under the rule of this most wicked of men. It wouldn't be life at all but a most miserable existence.

"By my honor," Brin spoke, "I feel I must warn you not to proceed with your intent. Things are not always as they appear. I shall give you the opportunity to surrender, for I carry a warrant for your arrest. As for your men, they shall be free because, to my knowledge, they have committed no crime as of yet. They may turn and leave, only never to return to the kingdom from which they hail, whether that be the kingdom of Peacehaven or the kingdom of Avery."

Lucian laughed heartily and said, "I know of a certainty you do indeed now jest. Know you not these kingdoms are as good as in my hand."

Brin replied, "Let not him that girdeth on his harness boast himself as he that putteth it off."

"Lucian," Karl interrupted, "this is folly, let us leave off this madness."

"Quiet!" Lucian snapped back to Karl.

"Are you still thus inclined?" Lord Brin asked, trying to give Lucian every opportunity to repent.

"Give me those children, *NOW!*" Lucian screamed, dropping all pretense and losing any measure of self-control.

Lord Brin answered, "If you want the children, you will have to take them." At that moment, Brin, Albert, and Johanan drew their swords as quick as lightning.

Karl tried one last time to stop what was about to take place, "I beg you, Lucian, do not do this thing!" But it was too late.

Lucian ducked behind the trees and called for the attack. In response to the command, Lucian's men began closing in on the trio. Abruptly, a shower of arrows came raining down on them from every direction. Lucian's men were stunned from the surprise assault, and many fell during the confusion. Karl leapt out of the way just in time, barely avoiding taking an arrow to the neck as he heard the whizzing sound and felt its wind. Realizing they were now the ones under attack, Lucian's men fought in desperation, and several managed to break through the barrage of arrows. Brin, Albert, and Johanan were now fighting back to back, wielding swords with a fury and working wondrously.

"I knew it!" Karl said to himself as he took shelter behind a rock. "I have followed this mad man right into a trap, but I refuse to fight for him."

There was no fear of battle in Karl, neither fear of death nor loss of limb, but something stronger than fear gripped this seasoned man of war. From deep within his own heart, the question that haunted him then was: *How could I have been so foolish?* Lucian had spun a deadly web of deceit, and now Karl felt hopelessly pressed out of measure, tightly tangled and ready to be devoured. Was it the greed of gold, lust for power, or simply pretentious pride that had led Karl so far astray? Maybe it was some alluring combination that preyed upon his human frailties, but what did that matter now?

"This has all turned to madness," he reasoned with himself. "I must find a way to redeem myself and right my wrongs." In the midst of the raging battle around him, it took more strength and courage for Karl to stay his sword than to engage in combat. So behind the rock, he hunkered down and listened intently to the sound of swords clashing, arrows flying, and men dying.

The woodsmen proved their worth and wonder many times over. Their bows twanged, and every arrow found its mark. Many of Lucian's army perished, yet there were plenty of men to fill the ranks of the fallen, but to no avail. Lucian's men spent their arrows for naught, for they shot wildly at their unseen enemy among the treetops. After the woodsmen's arrows were spent, it was time for the slingers to go to work. Many of Lucian's men fell in battle that day not knowing what hit them.

What a battle! As their weapons diminished, the woodsmen began to jump from the trees on top of their enemy. As defeat closed in upon Lucian's army, many began to desert their post only to find that they were surrounded. There was fighting before and fighting behind.

At the beginning of the battle the children stayed huddled together behind their rock. Eve did not dare to look, but Dawn couldn't stop herself and eventually peered out from the safety of their hiding place to keep a watchful eye on the action. Brin, Albert, and Johanan had fought back to back for some time, but now the battle was spreading farther apart.

Dawn carefully crawled up and out of the trench and could no longer see Brin and Johanan but positioned herself so as to have a good view of her father. *He is a marvelous warrior,* she thought to herself as she watched him fight so skillfully and unafraid. She was soon overtaken by a fresh new depth of love for the man she called "father," knowing he was fighting for her. He loved her so much he was willing to die to keep her safe. It was more than she could ever have hoped for.

Karl held his position behind the rock, determined not to engage in the clash. He realized the skirmish was quickly spreading as the woodsmen descended the trees. He decided to attempt retreat into the forest unnoticed if he could. Slowly, he began to crawl, sheltering himself behind the bodies of fallen soldiers until he made his way at last to the base of a huge tree not far from the old path. Here, he had a good view of the battlefield and could see what was taking place. *So that is the answer to the riddle,* he thought to himself. *That is Sir Marcus of Avery. Now I understand. That fool Lucian hasn't accounted for everything in the equation. Thus is the way with tyrants; their pride and greed blind their minds to reason and truth.*

The sounds of battle slowly began to fade, and Karl realized the fighting was nearly over. Still reeling from the events of the day, unsure of what to do or how to do it, Karl did not yet realize the crucial role he would play in this drama. Then movement nearby caught his eye. It was Lucian crawling on his belly like a cursed serpent. *Looking for a hole to slither into,* Karl thought. But that wasn't it at all. Lucian had picked up a bow from a fallen soldier and was now retrieving an arrow. The fighting had stopped. Lucian's army had been defeated.

"Give it up, Lucian!" Karl yelled. "It's over!"

"Not yet, it isn't!" came the hideous growl in response. And with that Lucian stood upright, put arrow to the string, and let it fly. At the same moment Karl heard the scream.

Standing beside the rock, Dawn was just about to run to her father when her keen eyes caught sight of movement at edge of the tree line. She saw a man put arrow to the string and realized her father was the intended target.

"Father! Look out!" she yelled with all her might. Then, without hesitation, she plunged headlong ahead of him to shield him from the arrow. The arrow struck with such force that Dawn's small frame was propelled through the air backward before landing with a thud and then folding limp like a rag doll.

Lord Albert wailed, "NO!!!" as he ran to her side.

Eve had emerged from her hiding place just as Dawn began to run and had witnessed the entire surreal event. She ran to her sister screaming, "Dawn! Dawn!" Albert was already cradling his little girl in his arms as Eve gently clasped the nearly lifeless hand that hung by her side.

Karl could hardly believe the remarkable scene that had just unfolded before his eyes. Without hesitation, he drew his dagger from his leather girdle and thrust it swiftly with all his might at the murderer. The blade found its mark, landing square between Lucian's eyes, and sinking deep into his forehead. He fell backward, as if in slow motion, the well-defined look of shock on his face as his lifeless body struck the ground, never to rise again.

Albert held his precious daughter, crying, "Dawn, Dawn, why did you do such a thing?"

In a weak voice she answered, "Please do not be angry with me, Father, for it was my purpose. Instead of you saving me, I was meant to save you all along. I am glad to fulfill it. And, please, do not mourn overmuch, for I go to that wonderful place where I shall meet my Lord. I go to be with my mothers, the one I knew while on earth, and to meet the one I never knew. Though I shall miss you, I love you, Father."

Eve found her voice and burst out, "Dawn, don't leave me! You can't leave me!"

"It looks as if I must," Dawn answered.

Through her tears Eve said, "But Dawn, we're sisters. I thought we'd be together forever."

As the color drained from Dawn's face her bright rosy cheeks slowly turned to an ashen grey. Her ragged little dress, the only one she owned, was now the color of crimson, soaked in blood. For a few fleeting moments she clung tightly to the silver thread within her, and then whispered ever so gently, "Don't you understand? We will be together forever. I'm just going down the long path before you. I'll be waiting by the stream. You'll find me."

Eve was sobbing now, "No! Dawn, no!"

Dawn struggled for breath as she said, "Remember, till you find me, you shall always carry a part of me with you — for we are sisters, secret sisters."

Eve said, "I love you, Dawn, my sister! My forever secret sister."

With her very last ounce of strength, Dawn looked into Albert's eyes one last time and said, "Goodbye, Father, I love you." She then looked at Eve and said, "I love you, Eve, my secret sister. Don't forget to meet me by the stream...." As she said this, her words trailed off, her head fell back, and her hand slipped from Eve's grasp.

Albert just held the small body and quietly cried as he rocked back and forth. Eve sobbed uncontrollably as her heart broke within her. Johanan stood with his head bowed with tears streaming down his face. Brin gently reached down and took Eve in his arms and held her tight as they all wept together.

Time stood still as the company mourned, and the woodsmen quietly gathered round stunned, in disbelief.

Finally, Lord Brin realized they were surrounded and looked up. There stood Gilbert with his hand on Lord Albert's shoulder, Artemas, and all the woodsmen, along with someone he didn't recognize quietly talking with Sir Marcus.

Lord Brin handed over the care of Eve to Johanan as the stranger and Sir Marcus approached.

"Lord Brin," Marcus started, "this is Karl of Avery. He was once a captain under my king's command until alliance was made with Lucian the snake. He now wishes to repent of said alliance. As proof of this, I have witnessed that it was his blade that ended our plight."

Kneeling, Karl said, "My Lord Brin, I cry you mercy. Before the battle, I had already repented and determined in my heart to try somehow to amend my wrongs and regain my honor. For at the beginning, Lucian showed himself a different man, one who had been wronged, and I fell under the spell of his much fair speech and promise of riches. As time wore on, I began to see the truth, but alas it was far too late. I had already fallen into his trap. To you, Lord Brin of Peacehaven, and Sir Marcus of Avery, I relinquish my sword. You may do with me as you deem fit for I refuse not to die." When his speech was finished, he bowed his head and presented his sword.

Brin replied, "Captain Karl, on behalf of the kingdom of Avery and of Peacehaven, we accept your sword. Yet you may wear it still, for I believe you may yet reclaim your full honor. By your actions, you have already reclaimed a great deal. I shall testify before your king that you did all in your power to prevent this battle and did not participate, yet you accomplished the most good by avenging the foe of us all, and especially of the young Princess Dawn, whom he slew. In return, it would be most helpful for Sir Marcus and all the woodsmen if you would appear before Ahyram, king of Avery, and declare unto him all of Lucian's treachery."

"With a very good will," Karl said. "If I can help these men return to their homes and families, I shall gladly do so. I declare this thing and at least restore me part of my honor, before I suffer my fate."

Sir Marcus replied, "Let's not give ourselves up to the gallows just yet. There may be more work before you."

With these kind words a slight smile and look of relief came upon Karl's face, for he felt as if the weight of the entire world had been lifted from his shoulders.

As Karl and Sir Marcus took their leave to continue their conversation, Karl asked him, "By the way, what did you do with those fifty men you took as we encamped by the forest border?"

"What fifty men?" came the confused reply. "We took no men. All we did was pelt you with acorns and hornets."

"But the bear tracks—" Karl started, when suddenly, out of nowhere, there came a roar loud as thunder that seemed to shake the earth. Everyone looked up, and there on a rocky precipice in the distant horizon stood the longhaired, long-bearded figure of a man waving goodbye to them.

"Why that's Nicolas, the hermit!" shouted Sir Marcus. Then after a long awkward silence, he looked at Lord Brin and said, "So maybe I wasn't the Bear King after all."

WHAT HAPPENED AFTER

So at last everyone made his way toward home, and we now come to the end of our story. Hereafter is a brief account of what followed....

Captain Karl returned to the kingdom of Avery where he stood humbly before King Ahyram and gave a complete confession. He explained in great detail the evil exploits of Lucian and fully exposed the true depth and nature of his treachery, thus clearing the woodsmen of all charges and fully restoring their good names. Lord Brin appeared before King Ahyram and gladly fulfilled his promise to testify on Karl's behalf. In like manner, with honor and dignity restored, Sir Marcus stood once more before his king and declared all the goodly acts of Karl and how, by his noble actions, they were delivered from the murderous hand of Lucian at the end of the battle. For his crimes, Karl was justly sentenced to help the woodsmen who had returned to rebuild or repair their homes and lands. King Ahyram also saw fit to strip him of his title and rank of "Captain," which made no matter, for Karl had begun to despise his position and found he was relieved to be loosed of it. He became known as Karl the Restorer, and he worked the rest of his days helping others with a thankful heart, enjoying the great mercy he had been shown.

Sir Marcus was promoted to Chief of the Royal Guard and given distinction to serve as personal protector to the king, which was quite an honor. King Ahyram addressed the stately assembly and said, "And who in all the kingdoms of the world can be found so faithful to the king as this? One who would suffer such wrong and yet remain loyal and true!"

As the ceremonies were ended and the court began to clear, Lord Brin seized the moment as he felt the Spirit bid him do, and thus turned to Sir Marcus and spoke as if to gently enter some unseen open door. "Indeed no one is more deserving than you."

Sir Marcus replied, "My thanks to you, Lord Brin. But, there is one small matter that has pressed upon me for days and now, I feel that it must needs be addressed for all to be complete."

"And what could that be?" asked Brin, knowing in his heart that this was truly a divine encounter, ordained of God.

"You promised to tell me more of this God of yours. For none can deny that it is He who has blessed such a wretch as I with so much grace and goodness. And for some time now I am most certain that I can hear Him calling my heart from within...."

Lord Albert returned to marry Cook. For he found that, try as he may in all his travels, he could hardly seem to close his eyes without the vivid memory of their first meeting that day at Lord Brin's cottage in Finnley Forest passing unexpectedly through his mind. Upon his return, Lord Albert wasted no time pursuing Cook and bold as a lion took the first opportunity to tell her all his heart. It was a glorious day that neither shall ever forget. For Cook, as it were, had rather taken quite a fancy to Albert and had cherished their first meeting in her own heart as well. Together, they resumed the work the late Queen Grace had started with the orphans of the great fever. This became the first orphanage ever in the kingdom of Peacehaven and was embraced with tender adoration by all who ever entered its happy halls. The children here were especially happy, healthy, and well-cared for. With the great Lord Albert and gentle Cook as their guides, they were without question the best educated and most well-rounded children in all the land.

Most importantly, it was a Christ-centered home overflowing with genuine Christian love. Many of these orphans grew to be great leaders in the kingdom, sensible men and women of renown, yet humble and hospitable in every sense of the word. Yes, Lord Albert and Cook left much good fruit. Lord Albert soon came to realize that Dawn's sacrifice afforded life and hope for scores of others. Her loving gesture of sacrifice had not only saved Lord Albert's life but also made a way for countless lives to be rescued.

Verily, verily, I say unto you, Except a corn of wheat fall into the ground and die, it abideth alone: but if it die, it bringeth forth much fruit. He that loveth his life shall lose it; and he that hateth his life in this world shall keep it to life eternal. Lord Albert took much comfort from these words and thought of them often.

Lord Albert also kept his word to Gilbert and started a contingent of slingers for the king's army. The legacy continues till this day. It is said that none can compare, except of course, the men of Avery.

Johanan was promoted to the position held by Lord Brin and became Captain Johanan. Though younger than many of the men he now commanded, he proved a worthy leader and soon gained the great respect of his men. Lord Brin was very proud indeed, for Captain Johanan behaved himself as a man much wiser than his years.

In the course of time, Johanan married a fine young maiden from the village of Garland where he had grown up, and their first child was a darling daughter they named Victoria Dawn. As she grew, Johanan gladly encouraged her love for the outdoors and taught her much about the value of love and life in the midst of Finnley Forest. It was there, like Dawn, where Victoria learned to find splendor and beauty in the everyday things surrounding her. Johanan loved Victoria with all his heart and through his own daughter never forgot that very special little girl who long ago had taught the young, all-knowing warrior so many valuable lessons.

Lord Brin was promptly promoted to the honorable position once held by Lucian, a place of such honor and nobility that King Amasa feared would never be filled again. Lord Brin became the most trusted advisor and best friend that King Amasa had ever known. His friendship proved true, and the advice he gave was as if from the very oracle of God. Lord Brin appointed a reeve to tend his own manor and business affairs, which had been neglected while caring for Eve and living within Finnley Forest. Upon advice from the king, Lord Brin situated himself inside the very castle itself, and was thereafter always near his beloved Eve. His worst fears proved unfounded, for he didn't lose her after all.

Although King Amasa was elated to have his daughter Eve home again, he grieved very deeply for the loss of Dawn. In a somber royal affair, she was buried beside her mother, Queen Grace, and the entire kingdom mourned her death for 30 days. At the end of 30 days, they held a feast in celebration to honor her life. This celebration they kept yearly and it became known as "Dawn's Day."

The King was very thankful for the fine upbringing Lord Brin and Cook had given Eve. They had taught her well and proved to be the best guardians possible for the young princess, for she had not grown spoiled and pampered, accustomed to having every desire catered to. Eve was a courtly young princess, thoughtful and humble, slow to speak yet filled with innocent charm.

Clearly she shall make a fine queen one day, King Amasa often thought to himself. He was also aware that even though he had his daughter back, in her heart, Lord Brin would always be her father. But he comforted himself knowing that to have her alive and well was after all a small price to pay. Through it all, Eve proved to have more than enough love for both fathers.

Eve grew into the most delightful young woman the kingdom had ever known; stunning in beauty yet in every way remarkably modest. Hardly a week went by that Eve didn't visit Cook, Lord Albert, and the children under their care. On her frequent visits, she showered the children with love and always took an abundance of treats, for which all of the children were most thankful. She loved to teach the older girls, as Cook had once taught her. While cooking, cleaning, and mending shirts all found their proper place, Eve was bold and full of adventure and soon discovered that she had a passion for sharing stories. She told of ships and sails and faraway places; stories of kings and kingdoms of old and even silly yarns to nurture the children's imaginations. But, there was nothing quite so special as when she told the tale of her and her sister, Dawn, and the day they first met by the stream, the day their lives changed forever. When she spoke of Dawn and their journey through Wylderland, such warmth and joy filled her heart that it seemed to set her face aglow. The children listened spellbound as the princess told of the scratch marks, the hanging bones, the hidden village, and how the men of Avery moved through the trees like ghosts. It was as if each time she told the tale she could take Dawn by the hand and relive every step of the journey all over again. It was such a wonderful story that no matter how oft she told it, on nearly every visit, the children would beg to hear it again and again.

After the death of good King Amasa, Eve was crowned Queen of Peacehaven and was adored by all the land. She ruled well with righteousness and honor. Queen Eve continued to follow the counsel of Brin, her father, till the end of his days.

During her reign, she renewed old alliances and friendships with the neighboring Kingdom of Avery, which occasioned the meeting of someone she had known several years earlier, except now he was known as Sir Mikael. He stood before her arrayed in full battle armor, strong, handsome, and proud.

"Mikael! Is that you? Is it really you?" She asked at their meeting.

"Yes, tis me, Your Highness, Sir Mikael, Captain of the host of archers of the Kingdom of Avery, at your service."

"But, good Sir, it seems you have forgotten something."

"Forgive me, I pray, forgotten what, Your Highness?"

"You were told to call me Eve," she said with a smile.

As one might expect in delicate matters such as these, in due time the seeds of affection took root and they fell hopelessly in love. Their union was no doubt providential in spirit but quite popular among the people as well. The wedding was so grand that nearly the entire kingdom was in attendance. Never had the land seen such a celebration, nor at any time since.

Together they ruled the land justly but wisely tempered, with an abundance of mercy. Queen Eve bore two sons; the first they named Brin Amasa, and the younger they named Marcus Albert. The entire kingdom rejoiced.

Then when good Queen Eve was old, full of days, and ready to make her final journey, she lay in her bedchamber surrounded by her children and grandchildren. The last words her family heard her say was not in the crackled voice of an old woman but rather in the voice of a young girl as they heard her say, "My Secret Sister, I have come at last."